CASTLE TERROR

CASTLE TERROR

Marion Zimmer Bradley

This title first published in Great Britain 1994 by
SEVERN HOUSE PUBLISHERS LTD of
9–15 High Street, Sutton, Surrey SM1 1DF.
First published in the USA 1994 by
SEVERN HOUSE PUBLISHERS INC., of
425 Park Avenue, New York, NY 10022.

British Library Cataloguing in Publication Data
Bradley, Marion Zimmer
 Castle Terror
 I. Title
 813.54.[F]

 ISBN 0-7278-4660-4

To My Mother

Typeset by Hewer Text Composition Services, Edinburgh.
Printed and bound in Great Britain by
Hartnolls, Ltd, Bodmin, Cornwall.

Chapter

One

AFTER THE comparative darkness of the train, the ripple of the water was blinding. The sun, striking the water high and aslant, broke the waves into millions of points of colorless dazzle. As I fumbled in my pocket for the sunglasses I hadn't expected to need, I felt the crackle of Mr. McLeod's telegram. I didn't really need the telegram; its directions were brief to the point of curtness, and I had memorized them within five minutes.

TAKE THE TRAIN WHICH ARRIVES AT 4:15, AND SOMEONE FROM SANCTUARY ISLAND WILL MEET YOU AT THE STATION AND BRING YOU TO THE ISLAND.

Sanctuary Island—the very name of the place seemed weighted with the strangeness of it all. I felt like pinching myself. Standing in the dazzle of the bright water, which shone even under the platformed overhang of the railroad station, I seemed to have stepped into a new and brilliant world from that gray and drab Philadelphia hospital where I had walked through the ragged, treadmill weeks of the past winter. Could I possibly be the same Susan Moore who had lain awake night after weary night, crying softly into her pillow because life seemed too hopeless? And yet, only yesterday, I had been nerving myself for the usual daily round, forcing myself to face Raymond—*Doctor Grantham,* I always had to remind myself—in the surgery that morning.

A sensible, practical woman—and what else should a nurse be, if not sensible and practical?—would have left the hospital and put an end to all the hopelessness.

It had been insane from the beginning. I had known he was married—happily married. But there's no explaining these things; all at once I had been madly, crazily in love with him, so that to look at him and know that when he looked back he saw nothing but my white uniform and black-striped cap was torture. But it would have been worse torture not to see him at all.

I had kept telling myself, feverishly, *It's only an infatuation, some trick of chemistry. Something about the way he walks, the glint of the sun on his blond hair, the serious, intent, and yet somehow sensuous line of his mouth.*

But it hadn't done any good. And finally it had broken. . . .

All the way up in the train, I'd been compulsively reliving that last interview. It was like biting on a sore tooth or being compelled to sit through a horror movie again and again, without even being able to get up and leave. There had been only one operation scheduled that morning, a routine tonsillectomy, and when he turned away from the scrub sink, he had said crisply, "Oh, Miss Moore; just a minute, if you please. Would you like to step into the doctors' lounge and wait for me?"

My heart had done something that the anatomy book said was impossible. Even though I knew, rationally, that he probably meant nothing but business, some outlaw hope inside me kept singing. This was the first time he had taken special notice of me.

When he came in, he had changed from the loose, sacklike scrub suit worn in surgery to the ordinary white-coat uniform he wore on his rounds. *There ought to be a law against men that handsome,* I thought bitterly; *it does hellish things to female chemistry.* I stood up, correctly, the way they taught us to do in nursing school when a doctor came into the room. He waved me down again and sat down comfortably on a sofa, his long legs stretched out, relaxed as a cat.

"Susan," he said abruptly, and I started, because it was not the formal "Miss Moore" that was his usual way of addressing me, "you're looking a little peakish lately."

Immediately, irrationally, I was on the defensive. "Have I been anything less than competent, Doctor Grantham?"

6

"No, no," he said quickly; "no one has any complaint to make. On the contrary, you seem—if anything—overly conscientious; but—something on your mind, Susan?"

I had two sudden, terrible, conflicting impulses—to cry or to blurt out, in one uncontrollable sentence, all my love and longing. Of course, I didn't do either. I swallowed hard and said, "Nothing that should affect my work, doctor."

"Personal trouble? If there was anything I could do . . ."

The solicitude hurt because I knew it was only the natural concern of a kind doctor for a good nurse. Without vanity, I knew I *was* a good nurse. But oh, the irony of that "If there was anything I could do. . . ." Because there wasn't. I'd been in his office. I'd seen the picture of Madeline Grantham on his desk, and the big triple-framed picture of the three little girls in pinafores and ponytails, ages four, three, and two.

Dr. Grantham was looking at me, still with the same kindly solicitude. "Nevertheless, you look as if you needed a vacation, or at least a change of air," he said; "in fact, I'm going to insist on it. Doctor's orders," he added, and suddenly the look on his face told me:

He knew. And my face was flooded, suddenly, with such scalding embarrassment that I could feel the heat down through the starched collar of my uniform. This was the oldest and the most foolish situation in hospital history—the nurse who becomes infatuated with the doctor.

He was still regarding me in a kindly, impersonal way. I set my teeth and took a hitch in my backbone.

"I am prepared to send in my resignation any time you say, doctor," I said stiffly.

"That's not exactly what I had in mind," he said. "I was looking over your record the other day, Susan, because of something that's recently come up. I understand that, although you've specialized here as a surgical nurse, you originally were a licensed psychiatric nurse, and you've worked in mental hospitals. Naturally, when this assignment offered itself, I thought right away of asking you."

7

"Assignment?"

"I got a letter the other day from a college friend of mine," he said. "It seems that his kid sister needs a nurse-companion. He didn't say exactly what was wrong with the girl, but for reasons he didn't specify, he thought it would be wise to have her attended by a psychiatric nurse. He emphasized that except for very rare spells, the nurse would be more of a companion than a nurse—in fact, they especially wanted someone young and pretty and cheerful, so that the girl wouldn't feel as if she were being placed under a jailer or a keeper. They wanted someone who could amuse her and keep her cheered up. They live on a beautiful island—I visited there once when I was in prep school, though I haven't seen Brant since college—and I gather that most of the time it would be almost more of a vacation than a serious nursing assignment. My guess is that the girl's had a nervous breakdown, but I'm not sure. Anyhow, why don't you think it over? I called Brant McLeod and told him I had exactly the girl in mind. I was pretty sure you'd accept. A little sea and sunshine should do you a world of good," he added persuasively.

I felt almost paralyzed by conflicting impulses. It *was* a way out—and yet, it meant that he was getting rid of me. Or was he merely giving me a way of escape from an impossible situation?

"Promise me you'll at least think it over, Susan," he said; and then, almost as if the words were being forced out against his will, he added, "It would do me good—to think of you being out of this rat race here. For purely selfish reasons . . ."

He broke off as if he had said more than he'd meant to say. And yet, suddenly, the knowledge broke over me like a wave—the danger was there for him, too. This gave us both a reasonable, dignified way of escape. A clean break would remove us both from temptation.

"I don't need to think it over," I said; "it sounds wonderful. I've thought, sometimes, of getting back into psychiatric nursing."

The look in his eyes—relieved and grateful—told me all I needed to know. He might very well have offered me

8

his hand, but he didn't, and I knew why. I knew, as if with a sixth sense, that if he'd touched my hand we'd have been in each other's arms. He stood up and said, "Fine. I'll give you the address, and you can telephone McLeod this afternoon. Good luck—Susan."

Then I'd found myself watching him walk out of the room, realizing blurrily that I'd probably never see him again. After a while I had made myself get up and go down to the nurses' station to tell the nurse in charge that Dr. Grantham was arranging to send me out on a private case.

When I'd called later, I hadn't spoken to Brant McLeod. I'd spoken to an impersonal voice that identified himself as McLeod's private secretary and said, Oh yes, I was the girl Dr. Grantham had recommended, and Mr. McLeod would send me a telegram about arrangements, if I could come at once, preferably tomorrow.

The rest of the day had been spent in whirlwind arrangements that left me too busy to think—packing; arranging to give up my apartment and board my cocker spaniel, Cricket, at a kennel; notifying the milkman, the post office, and my small circle of friends. I had told them only that it was a new job. That was a nurse's life for you, I told them, and they hadn't asked questions.

The terse telegram with instructions had come. That night I had been too exhausted with preparations even to cry into my pillow.

And now, here I was, standing on the shore, still feeling numbed, as if under an anesthetic. But I realized slowly, as the brightness of the water brought me out of it, that I had been lucky to get away in time, before I made a fool of myself or Dr. Grantham. For instead of *being* a psychiatric nurse, I had *needed* one.

There were several small boats tied up at the dock, and I walked the length of the platform to have a closer look at them. A tall man, sun glinting on his fair hair, turned around, and for a moment there was that catch in my throat again; sun on fair hair—like Dr. Grantham's! But then I saw that the man's sunburned features were nothing at all like Dr. Grantham's fine ones. This man looked as if he spent all his time outdoors; he wore khaki work pants and an open-collared shirt to match, and his hands were big and calloused.

"Were you looking for someone, Miss? The stationmaster can probably help you. Or did you want to hire a boat?"

"I'm expecting to be met," I said, and he raised well-bred eyebrows. "Where are you going?"

"Sanctuary Island," I said, and he nodded. "I thought so, perhaps. I live there, myself—though I expect you're going to Duncarlie Castle."

"I'm working for some people named McLeod."

"That will be the Castle," he confirmed. There was a faint trace of a Western drawl in his speech; I wondered where he came from, then realized with amazement that this was the first time I'd shown even transient interest in any man other than Raymond in months. Not that I was interested in this blond man in khaki who looked and sounded like a cowboy. But I had *noticed* him. I *had* stepped into a new world!

He was looking fixedly at someone behind me with an intensity that made me turn, and I saw an old man in dungaree pants and a checkered bandanna approaching us. He was stooped, and he limped slightly. The old man stumped around me stiff-kneed and looked up with a stare that would have been rude if it had been less frank.

"You'll be the nurse lady for Duncarlie Castle, Miss?"

"I am Susan Moore."

"The nurse lady, yes. Mr. Brant telephoned in and told me to pick you up and take you out to Sanctuary Island. Where's your baggage, Miss? I'll get that stationmaster person to stow it on my boat."

"Ah, yes," the blond man said, "Brant did mention a nurse. Look here, Jim," he said to the old man, "I can spare you a trip out. Unless Miss Moore has forty suitcases, she'll fit very well in my speedboat, and I'm ready to start back for Sanctuary in ten minutes." He smiled engagingly at me. "When Martine told me she'd engaged a keeper for Deirdre, I'd pictured some icy-faced old battle-ax, and I'd figured to crawl into my hole and pull it in after me. But under the present conditions it will be a pleasure to give you a lift out there and save old Jim a trip."

10

The old man scowled. He said truculently, "I takes my orders from the old gentleman, Hunter, and Mr. McLeod told me to bring Miss Moore and her luggage out to Sanctuary Island. You tend to your birds, or whatever it is you do out there, and let me tend to my business. If you'll step this way, Miss Moore—"

"Now wait a minute," the blond man—Hunter?—said. For a minute they were actually squared off as if they would come to blows. The contrast was almost laughable, between the tall, young cowboy type and the gnarled old man, but there was something grim and deadly serious about it, too.

I said, ineffectually, "Oh, please—"

"I has my orders, Miss," said the old man implacably; "you're to come with me. The old gentleman, Mr. McLeod, won't like it elseways."

Hunter smiled, a mere baring of his teeth. "And of course the old gentleman's wishes are sacred? What do you say, Miss Moore?"

I hesitated. "I suppose . . . Mr. McLeod is my boss—"

Smiling pleasantly, he said, "And of course you know nothing at all about me. I might be a thug, a hooligan, a murderer, a rapist. No doubt I'll see you on the Island, Miss Moore." With exaggerated courtesy, he made a little gesture which made me think—though he was hatless—of tipping his hat in Western style, and turned away. The old man glowered after him.

"Who was that?" I asked, but old Jim took no notice.

"If you'll step this way, Miss. How much luggage do you have?"

I pointed out my two suitcases and the dressing bag. Grunting brief approval, he hoisted them neatly and jerked his head toward the dock. A fourteen-foot inboard motorboat, painted neatly blue and white, was tied there. Old Jim stowed my luggage and held out his hand to help me step carefully into the swaying boat. I sat down, closing my eyes against the redoubled glint of sun on water. I suddenly realized that I hadn't been in a motorboat since school days, and the thought of living on an island stirred old, romantic, dreams. I had been working too hard. I had

11

taken too little time to relax, to swim and sail and enjoy life.

Old Jim pointed to the light coat over my arm. "Better put that on, Miss. It gets cool on the water toward sunset."

Obediently I buttoned it up to my chin; but the wind, as the motor roared into life, felt good in my hair. The sun turned the water a dozen shades of gold and orange.

I asked, "How far is it to the island?"

"Three, four miles off the mainland. I hope you'll be staying, Miss. The last young lady they had, she wouldn't stay. *She* wanted shops and the movies close at hand, I have no doubt. Frivolous, she was, and no mistake. And the one before that—just after poor Miss Margo was killed —well, Mr. Brant wouldn't have her around at any price. Proper old devil she was. I'd be sorry myself for poor little Miss Deirdre if that old harridan was looking after her. So I'm hoping you'll stay awhile, Miss Moore. Poor, pretty little thing Miss Deirdre is, or used to be. Nobody sees her now, but a sweet little thing she used to be, coming down and begging Old Jim for boat rides. I'd take her round the island, and she'd be pleased as if she'd been to London to visit the Queen." Grimly, he pulled at the starting handle, and the motor roared into life.

For a few minutes I lost myself in the whipping feel of the wind roaring past my ears; then I heard Old Jim speak again.

"Your first visit to Duncarlie Castle, Miss?"

"I didn't even know it was a castle," I said, intrigued.

"You'll find it lonely there, maybe," he warned, "unless you like it that way. The mailboat stops there twice a week, and the servants come in one night a week to do their shopping, but from one year's end to the other, nobody sees the folk from the Castle. Oh, Mr. Brant comes to the mainland now and then on business, and Mrs. Mc-Leod comes sometimes for shopping. But the old gentleman, *he* hasn't left Duncarlie Castle in seven years or more. Poor old gentleman, with all them harpies just waiting for him to die, just fastened on him, sucking his blood like leeches. And poor little Miss Deirdre—nobody ever sees her any more."

I realized that according to the ethics of my profession,

12

I was wrong to encourage this gossip, but his mysterious hints had awakened my curiosity. "I've never even been in this part of the world before. I don't know anything about Sanctuary Island, or about the Castle."

"Then you won't be knowing—no, of course not." His voice, raised above the roar of the motor and the wind, had a curious, harsh stridency. "Back a hundred years or so, in my grandfather's time, they say old Mr. McLeod came over from Scotland and made himself a fortune in some way or other and brought over the ancestral castle, stone by stone—cost him millions, they do say—and set it up here on Sanctuary Island."

I had heard of eccentric millionaires doing that in the nineteenth century, but I'd never believed I would actually see such a place.

"The McLeods have always kept themselves to themselves, but they came and went to the mainland until just a few years ago." He hesitated, then glanced sideways at me, his eyes bright. "No doubt I shouldn't be telling you all this, Miss; it might make you not want to stay—if you're the nervous type."

"Heavens, no," I laughed; "what is it, an ancient Scottish ghost that walks the castle battlements every night playing his bagpipes?"

At his offended frown I quickly apologized. "Please do forgive me; I wasn't making fun—"

"No ghosts that *I* know of," he reproved me somberly, "but if there were, there'd be good reason. Seven years ago, or such like, they found a dead man there—lying on the beach." His voice fell to that curious, harsh, strident whisper. "His body was hacked to pieces, *and his face was gone!* They never did find out who he was, nor what happened to him, and there were some people came snooping round accusing the McLeods—as if people like *them* would have anything to do with murder," he added, glowering at me as if I'd accused his cherished employers of personally dismembering the unidentified man.

I felt a curious little *frisson* of fear, which I knew was completely irrational; after all, I'd been a nurse four years, and I'd seen accident victims and corpses mutilated in all sorts of ways.

13

"My guess is that some gang of criminals took somebody out for a ride," the old man said, "and left him there, hoping the body wouldn't be found. Maybe they thought it was one of the deserted islands—they left him on the sea side, where all the sea caves are, and the Castle's on the mainland side of the island. But there were reporters, and police, and newspapermen, and since then the McLeod family have cut themselves right off. The place is pointed out to tourists, but that's all anyone knows about it." He swerved the boat's tiller to the right and pointed with his free hand. "Yonder it lies—Duncarlie Castle, Miss."

The sunset turned the water to pale, shimmering gold. Above it, the sky had paled to a colorless gray, and against this grayed blue I saw, rising ahead of me, fantastic spires and turrets. . . .

I said, stupidly, "It's a real castle!"

"I told you. The old gentleman's grandfather had it brought over, stone by stone. To be sure it's a real castle."

It looked like something from a picture in my book of fairy tales—grim; cold; changeless and ageless. It was certainly not anything people would actually live in, would go to sleep and get up and eat and drink—and hire psychiatric nurses—in! It was black and forbidding against the sky.

The boat slowed as we entered the Castle's shadow, and I felt the dark loom over me, even though, as we neared the shore, I could see that it was set back perhaps a quarter of a mile, atop a hill, and that there were sparse woods between the shore and the castle. Suddenly, with a twinge of fear, I felt reluctant to set foot on Sanctuary Island. The gruesome story of the dead man with no face, the grim, fantastic old castle, even the old-world speech of the old man at my side, combined to make me shudder. But even as I struggled to overcome it, Old Jim was making the boat fast in a landing slip, and a man in a blue-chambray work shirt and jeans was anchoring the rope and bending down for my suitcases. And behind him a tall figure stood smiling, fair hair catching the last gleam of the sun, a blond man in khaki work clothes. He held out his hand.

14

"My speedboat is a little faster, Miss Moore, and I'm here to see Brant on business. I can show you the way up to the Castle. Don't worry about your luggage."

"Mr. Hunter!" I said, startled, letting him steady me as I stepped on shore.

"At your service," he nodded. "Welcome to Sanctuary Island."

Behind me I heard Old Jim mutter, ". . . him and his conniving, canoodling ways!"

"As a matter of fact," Hunter said pleasantly, "Brant asked me to show you up to the house. You can see about the luggage, Jim. This way, please, Miss Moore."

The boathouse and landing slips had everything necessary, and there were several small boats tied up at the dock. From there we stepped onto a green, shaded path that led upward. It was incredibly quiet after the roar of the motorboat, the noise of the train, the always-present background roaring of a big city. The only sounds were the faraway mutter of a speedboat and a soft, warbling sound of birds singing. I breathed in the fragrant, woodsy scent, and suddenly I felt the weight on my heart dissolve. It was peaceful here.

Beside the path there was the bright flash of a blue wing, and I cried out, briefly, with pleasure. The man named Hunter said, "The island really is a bird sanctuary, you know. Except for the part owned by the McLeod family, the rest of the island is government land, and there are thousands of birds that winter here. I'm the ranger here— my name is Ross Hunter, by the way—and mainly my job is to make sure no one bothers the wildlife. It's a paradise for a bird watcher. Are you, by any chance, interested in birds, Miss Moore?"

"I'm afraid I don't know much about them."

"You will," he promised. He seemed suddenly to prick up his ears at a slight sound, although all I heard was a birdsong—and indeed, during all the time I spent on Sanctuary Island, through the stormy passions and the terrors and the tempests, there always seemed to be a framework of peaceful birdsong.

As I turned to follow his eyes, I caught a glimpse of sun-

15

set glinting on a whisk of blue skirt, on a thin, white arm that was just disappearing into the woods. A girl? Whoever it had been, she was gone.

Ross said grimly, "Deirdre. They're crazier than she's supposed to be if they let her run around like that!"

A thousand questions trembled on my tongue. Ross was an intimate of the Castle. He could answer. . . . But the ethics of my profession, not to mention common courtesy, dictated that I wait for details from my employer.

Suddenly we were out of the woods and in the very shadow of the castle, in the overhang of a vast, heavy door. I hesitated, with a twinge of reluctance, but Ross stepped up with the familiarity of long knowledge and pressed a small button that was an anachronism against the gray stone of the wall. Very far away, muffled by intervening stone walls, I heard the sound of a bell.

Chapter

Two

THE DOOR opened slowly, with such an air of ceremony that it would hardly have surprised me to be greeted by a couple of men in medieval armor—or by the Fish-footman in *Alice's Adventures in Wonderland!* Instead, against the dimness that was the hall inside, a tall and angular woman stood waiting for us.

Her face was thin and narrow; her dark hair, drawn tightly back into a bun over tight temples, was already graying. Her features were those of a lady, but the dark, uniformlike dress, with plain white collar and cuffs and small satin apron, proclaimed her an upper servant of some kind. Her voice was low and expressionless.

"Mr. Hunter. Come in, please. Mr. Brant will be back in a few minutes." Then, catching sight of me, she smiled slightly. "Miss Moore?"

I admitted it, and she stepped back in a gesture of invitation and welcome. "I'm *very* glad to see you," she said, and to my surprise, the expression in her face and voice was actually one of relief and pleasure. "Matthew . . ."

A young man in a dark, plain suit came forward and relieved Ross of my luggage. The tall woman said, "I am Mrs. Meadows, the housekeeper. Mr. Brant McLeod left instructions that you were to be shown to your room. If you'll come with me, please? Matthew, have Miss Moore's luggage taken to the northwest tower room." Her glance dismissed Ross Hunter as she said, "You know your way into Mr. Brant's study. You can wait there, if you like."

His murmured thanks was impeccable, but he cast me an amused glance of irony. It was all too obvious that Mrs. Meadows didn't really care whether he liked it or not.

17

"This way, Miss Moore. I'm afraid there are rather a lot of stairs."

"That won't bother me, after a hospital," I said, and followed her.

My first impression of the inside of Duncarlie Castle was of dark luxury, almost overwhelming in its gloomy splendor. The hall was papered with an antique brocade pattern in dark green and gold, and there were brocade hangings; the only light came from a window at the far end, set with lozenge-shaped patterns in colored glass. The carpets were deep and dark underfoot, and on the stairs rich, dark carpeting muffled the sound of my heels. The housekeeper moved silently ahead of me, up two flights of stairs and along a long corridor, turning twice. I said inanely to her back, "How on earth will I find my way around?"

"It may be a little confusing at first," she said. She turned, and to my surprise the grim face held kindliness and even humor. "But you'll soon get used to it," she went on. "I do hope you'll like it here, Miss; poor little Miss Deirdre needs someone young around her. But a lady— not like that last young snippet of a girl we had! She said the place got on her nerves! Hmph! Nothing but the big city would have suited that one, and we were all glad enough to see her go back there."

This seemed to need comment, so I said, "It seems very beautiful here. And I think I'll enjoy the quiet."

"Quiet, it surely is. And you'll soon find your way around, though goodness knows the place wasn't built for convenience. I understand that in the olden days they didn't even have running water, and it was old Mr. Alexander who had modern conveniences put in. Nowadays, of course, you can't get a cook to stay without a modern kitchen and goodness knows what-all else!"

I asked, "Have you been here very long?" for she sounded like the old family retainer out of some novel.

But as if reading that thought, she smiled. "Oh, dear, no; only about five or six years. Old Mr. Jerome had all new servants after—" she broke off, and mentally I supplied, *after the murder*; but after a moment's pause, hardly a break, she went on, "—about eight years ago.

18

"Here is your room, Miss."

The room had the same movie-set unbelievability as the rest of the house—dark brocade hangings, deep green, traced with gold; a carved four-poster bed; carpets deep enough to swim in. I moved through it in amazement, wondering if it were really there, or just painted on.

Mrs. Meadows flicked a switch. "Light," she said in a crisp, practical voice, and somehow their quite ordinary electric brilliance made the whole thing seem more believable. She pulled a cord, and the draperies glided back to a view of sunlit ocean. "And your bath is here." The bath was more nearly modern than the rest of the house, although the tub was an ancient, footed model, and the washstand looked like marble. But were these servants' quarters? Or did they believe that a nurse-companion was entitled to the privileges of a guest?

A telephone rang from the bedside table. Startled, I picked it up and tentatively said, "Hello?"

An urgent male voice said, "Is Mrs. Meadows there, please?"

She was already at my elbow; she took the phone and listened for a moment, and then a look of distress slid over her features. She said, "Right away, Mr. McLeod," and replaced the receiver. "I'll have to leave you," she said hurriedly; "I'll send one of the maids to unpack."

"Please don't bother—"

"Mr. McLeod would wish it, Miss," she said inflexibly. As she hurried out the door, it slid shut noiselessly.

My suitcases already stood in the middle of the floor. I walked to the window and looked down at the curve of the green shoreline. Birds were dipping gracefully along the waterside, and at one point there seemed to be a low, flat, sandy beach, where the waves rolled in gently. This side of the island seemed to be sheltered; it was without surf. It looked as if there would be swimming. Far out on the darkening water, I saw the white gleam of a sail.

"Shall I unpack for you now, Miss Moore? My name is Carla."

I turned to see a colored girl in a dark dress like the housekeeper's, with the same white collar and cuffs, standing apologetically in the doorway. She said, "I did knock, but the walls are so thick here . . ."

"That's all right. Come in. Really, they needn't have bothered."

"No bother at all, Miss Moore. Mrs. McLeod said we were to do all we could to make you comfortable." She was already unfolding my dresses, hanging them in the closet, and stowing my nightgowns and underwear in the bureau drawers with easy, practiced hands. I felt vaguely abashed at their modesty against the luxury of these cedar-scented closets and drawers.

Carla held up a gray chiffon dress I usually saved for concerts and special dates. "Shall I press this for dinner, Miss?" she asked.

I hesitated. "I'd thought perhaps I should change into uniform—"

"No, Miss Moore; Mr. Brant wants to see you in the library, and he wanted you to join them at dinner tonight." Carla was already unfolding a small ironing board, and I gave way without protest. She probably knew more than I did about what was customary in a place like this! I certainly seemed to have fallen into the lap of luxury.

When I was ready I surveyed myself with unusual criticism in the long, gilt-framed pier glass on the closet door. Normally a mirror was something to make sure my cap was pinned on straight. But tonight, in these unbelievable surroundings, I felt strange. It seemed that the mirror must give back something new and strange as well. I began to realize that during the last several months I had begun to think of myself as a sort of uniformed female robot. Yet against this background, the mirror gave back a new image. The gray dress seemed to give a tinge of gold to the hair I usually thought of as dishwater blond. Perhaps it was excitement that made my cheeks glow and my eyes seem more blue than gray. Perhaps it was just the general fairy-tale atmosphere around me that made me feel as if I were dressed in cobweb and clouds and floating somewhere above the floor.

I felt considerably less secure when I ventured out of my room, even though the quiet-spoken Carla had given me careful directions. The corridors were wide and empty and deserted; yet I had the sense of someone watching me. Small, faraway sounds were muffled—the sound of a piano playing, and somewhere (surely I was mistaken!) the cry of a child, quickly hushed again. I hesitated at the foot of the stairs, turned and guessed at the correct door, and stepped back, hesitantly; I had blundered into a sort of pantry, lined with shelves. A tall old man with white hair raised his eyebrows as I stepped inside, and I blunderingly explained who I was.

He never batted an eyelash. "You took the wrong turning at the foot of the stairs," he informed me gravely. "If you'll come this way, I believe Mr. McLeod is waiting for you in the library."

Feeling reproved, I followed him across the hall and into a high-ceilinged room whose walls were lined with dark books. There was a grand piano here, and above it a framed portrait of a woman in costume, with a high Spanish ruff about her white throat and features of impeccable classic beauty. Her dark, magnificent hair was massed atop a finely shaped head. I stood for a moment admiring the portrait.

"My wife," said a dry voice from the shadows, and I turned to see a small old man in a wheelchair, who I knew must be Jerome McLeod. His face was as dry and lined as his voice. "It was painted in honor of her first performance as Princess Eboli in *Don Carlo,* at La Scala opera house. Perhaps you have heard the name of Martine Clereau?"

No opera fan, I; but I had heard the name. Who could avoid it?

"Martine has now retired from public life. We live very quietly here on Sanctuary Island, Miss Moore; I hope it will not be dull for you. Unfortunately, our last nurse found it so."

"It is very beautiful," I said; "I think I shall enjoy the quiet."

"I hope so—my stepdaughter is unfortunately in no position to leave the island, so that your life will be, of necessity, rather confining.

"Lowden?" The old man spoke without raising his voice.

The tall butler came forward quietly with a tray. "Sherry, Miss Moore?"

"Thank you." I accepted the glass.

"Ah, here you are, my dear," the man in the wheelchair exclaimed, as the door opened and a woman in a deep crimson gown swept into the room.

In a flash of shocked recognition, I knew she was the woman of the portrait—but how changed! Not by age, for this woman was still young; in fact, she could hardly be past her middle thirties. Was she actually married to the elderly wreck in the wheelchair? He must be seventy, at the very least! It was the same woman—unquestionably the same—and yet unbelievably different. Beauty was still there—or at least the haggard remains of what must once have been great beauty—and *chic* breathed from every line of her gown, which must have come from one of the great designers and which made my own gray chiffon look like bargain-basement stuff, which it wasn't. But the face was thin, tense, somehow ravaged as if by powerful emotion. Emotion kept under iron control, so that the eyes seemed to burn behind a frozen mask of haggard beauty.

"Miss Moore, my wife."

"How do you do, Mrs. McLeod."

She spoke some conventional phrase. The voice was deep and thrilling; I could well believe that this woman had been one of the great operatic contraltos of her day. Her every motion seemed theatrical, somehow larger than life. Yet she was only a slender woman, with thick, dark hair drawn into a Psyche knot above a low-cut dinner dress, matter-of-factly accepting a sherry from the butler's tray. She turned to me and said, "Doctor Grantham gave you most excellent references, Miss Moore. You know that you are to take complete charge of my daughter, Deirdre?"

"So I gathered. If I might know a bit more about her—"

"I'll leave that to Brant," Martine McLeod interrupted, almost rudely; "this is his idea." The harsh, impatient words were strangely at variance with the deep thrill that lay behind the voice. "Just let me warn you, Miss Moore, not to be too deceived. The girl may appear reasonably

22

normal at times. But for your own good I warn you—don't be taken in by her beautiful, false little face! She could convince anyone of anything—lunatics are clever, are they not?" Her brusque manner challenged me to deny it.

I extemporized, "Some mentally abnormal persons can seem quite plausible, yes."

"Just be careful not to believe a word she says," Martine repeated, "Particularly, she'll probably try to convince you that I—"

"Martine." It was a brief word, gently spoken, from the old man in the wheelchair. But Martine McLeod fell instantly silent. I was left puzzled, studying her. I had known many parents who felt strongly ambivalent toward an abnormal child. Some parents who were convinced that they loved their mentally defective children actually rejected them with something very like hatred. Was this the case with Martine? Or did that brusque manner actually cover a pain too great for speech? Had the tragedy of her daughter's abnormality robbed this once-beautiful woman of her beauty? And what was wrong with the girl, anyhow?

"Are we too late for some sherry?" It was the good-humored voice of Ross Hunter, who came striding into the library. Oddly enough, his khaki work clothes did not jar, but made the rest of us look overdressed. "How lovely you look, Martine. Good evening, Mr. McLeod, sir. Don't bother with introductions . . ." he turned to me, "Miss Moore and I met on the dock this afternoon, and poor old Jim practically fought me off with bared fists when I offered to run her out here myself in the speedboat."

Martine said, deep laughter in her voice, "The poor old fellow probably needed the money for the trip, Ross."

"No; he was only obeying orders," said a new voice, a deeper voice, and I saw, for the first time, the man who had entered the library behind Ross. He stood there, silent, a sherry glass held firmly between his fingers, and yet from that moment he seemed to dominate the entire scene, so that all the rest of them—the easy-mannered Ross, the flamboyant Martine, the dry old man in the wheelchair—faded out, as supernumeraries on the stage do when the star enters. It wasn't that he was handsome—I never knew

23

anyone who thought Brant McLeod handsome. He was somewhat over medium height, with powerful shoulders and a compact, rather rigid neck; his face seemed rugged in repose, the dark eyebrows almost meeting over his dark eyes, and his hair, which was thick and dark, falling low on his forehead; he might have been some ancient Roman, even to the sullen look which the sculptors of Roman coins gave to their Caesars. But he had something of the same air of command.

"I told Old Jim to bring Miss Moore here. Why on earth should you try to interfere with my orders, Ross?"

Ross actually hesitated a moment. Then the wit and repartee came back. "Why 'make a Federal case out of it, Brant? I just thought I'd save the old fellow a run—and after all"—he made a slight, gallant bow in my direction— "doesn't a reason suggest itself?"

Brant McLeod paid no attention. He was studying me with an air of silent concentration. But what he finally said was inconsequential. "We want you to feel quite at home, Miss Moore."

"When will I see my patient?"

"Tomorrow will be quite time enough," he replied, waving my question quickly aside. "Mrs. Meadows tells me—"

But what Mrs. Meadows had told him, I never knew; for at this moment Lowden announced that dinner was served, and came to wheel the old man's chair into the adjoining dining room.

The meal, though formal, was less so than I had feared. Ross talked over some obscure business with Brant, largely about migratory birds; Martine attempted small talk with me about the weather and the sea at this time of year, though I could tell she was not at home with it; the old man applied himself in silence to his food. At the conclusion of the meal, Lowden returned to wheel the old man back into the library, and Martine, lighting a cigarette, tapped Ross lightly on the shoulder.

"We have some new records that I ordered from New York; would you like to come and hear them?"

As I began to rise with the others, Brant McLeod

24

stopped me with a peremptory gesture. "Wait a moment, Miss Moore," he said; "I want to talk with you."

I reseated myself. Now, perhaps, I would hear about my patient. Over the candlelight of the table, flickering on his dark face, shadows seemed to come and go on Brant McLeod's features. He seemed reluctant to speak. Finally he asked, "How much did Ray Grantham tell you about Deirdre?"

"Almost nothing," I replied truthfully, "except that you felt it necessary to have a psychiatric nurse in attendance. Frankly, Mr. McLeod, I'd like a few more details."

He sighed. "I suppose it's inevitable," he said, and his mouth was set in a bitter line. "It seems to be up to me. There's no one else to care."

I was silent. What was there to say? Obviously the girl's mother was not going to be helpful.

He lighted a slim cigarillo; then he glanced at me for permission. "Forgive me—I'm accustomed to lighting up when Martine's out of the room. You don't mind?"

I liked cigar smoke and told him so, and he drew on the cigarillo for a moment without speaking. Then, resolutely, he leaned forward on the table.

"Deirdre is only my stepsister," he said. "She's Martine's daughter; my father married Martine when Deirdre was a little tyke of four or five. I used to carry her around on my shoulders—you don't want to hear about that. The point is, I'm fond of the child, and I want someone who will be a friend to her. Not just a nurse or, God forbid, a jailer."

I burst out, "I don't know whether the girl is an idiot or a raving maniac, Mr. McLeod."

"Neither," he said gravely. "She was a normal, bright, sunny little girl until she was nine years old—that was seven years ago. Then, something happened. *What,* we've never known. There was trouble on the island about that time—perhaps you've heard; if I know Old Jim, he'll have told you our local horror story."

"He said there had been a murder," I said cautiously.

"Yes. One of the islands near here belongs to someone who was a big-name bootlegger in the thirties"—he mentioned a name that even I knew—"and I suppose some of his hoodlums got out of hand. But the place was alive with police and newspapermen. I suppose the governess we had for Deirdre and little Jerry—that's my father's son by Martine—was too busy to see what was happening to the girl. Anyhow, one day Deirdre disappeared, and we found her one day in one of the sea caves—huddled up like a little wild animal. No one could get near her—she clawed and bit old Lowden, even, when he tried to carry her to the house, and even I couldn't calm her down. Martine couldn't begin to handle her. And she couldn't talk. We got a doctor from the mainland, finally—it had taken Lowden and myself and two of the footmen to get her into the house—to give her a sedative. And when she came around, she couldn't talk. Not a word.

"She didn't say a word for three years."

I stared in silent dismay. "And you have no idea what happened?"

"We've had a dozen ideas," Brant McLeod said grimly, "none of which any of us can prove. She wasn't sexually molested—that was the first thing we thought of, of course. But she was simply a little wild animal. She calmed down, after a while—or rather, she was tamed down. But she didn't speak for three years. When she began to talk again —quite suddenly—she had forgotten everything, even her own name. Complete amnesia. We tried everything —psychiatry, doctors everywhere—but nothing helped." He shrugged, wearily. "So we don't want her in an institution. She's a happy little girl who lives from day to day. She's really quite docile, except for occasional tantrums."

He sighed, then continued, "We had hopes, when she began to talk again, but they were useless. We got a companion for her—a young nurse named Margo Fields— but she died in an accident, about six months ago." A shadow passed over his face. "It was hard on Deirdre. Then we tried a—a regular nurse, but she was too harsh on the poor child. Deirdre began to regress and have tantrums all the time. Finally, we decided to try and get a psychiatric nurse—one who was young and could be a friend and companion to her, but who would know what to do if she suddenly—" he hesitated, and a spasm came over his face—"if she became—violent. The alternative

—well, I don't want her put in an institution. She'd wither up and die there," he said harshly. "I won't have it. You're our last chance, Miss Moore."

He really cares, I thought, looking at the mobile, sullen face in the shifting candlelight. He cared.

And what about my patient?

According to Martine, Deirdre was a falsely sweet psychopathic liar. According to Brant, she was a sunny, happy child who lived from day to day. And the housekeeper had called her "Poor little Miss Deirdre."

But what was the truth?

Brant McLeod rose abruptly. "You've had a long trip," he said; "you must be tired. I'll take you to Deirdre tomorrow; she's fond of me, and I'd better introduce you. Good night."

I went to my room in a daze. The castle seemed to overwhelm me suddenly, and my brocaded room seemed only a backdrop for the remorseless strangeness of the people around me. There was old Jerome McLeod, dry and embittered; Martine, with her operatic voice and her ravaged beauty and her cold bitterness toward her daughter; Ross, who came and went as if he owned the place; and finally, Brant, the enigma—by turns curt and solicitous.

I undressed, appreciating the luxury of the hot bath, the thick soft towels, and the deep rug under my bare feet. Someone had placed a bowl of luscious fruit beside my bed. I got into bed, biting into a pear that dripped sweet juice. Tomorrow I would meet Deirdre, my riddle of a patient. What had changed a "sunny, happy child" into a speechless, biting little animal?

I turned out the light. As my head hit the pillow, I realized that I had not thought of Raymond Grantham all day, that suddenly I had no desire to cry with tormented love and longing. The moon shone through the green-gold drapery at the window. I slept.

Some small sound disturbed me; abruptly, I sat up in bed. My own voice sounded strange in the darkness, as I asked, "Who's there?"

Silence. Through the dimness I made out the pale form of a slender, feminine body, dimly outlined in white drapery, moonlight sketching pale shadows around the shoul-

27

ders like fair hair. I said, more sharply, "Who's there?"

Dazed, I rubbed my eyes; then, resolutely, I reached for the switch of the light. It seemed to me that I heard a little cry, but I have never been sure. Then the light snapped on; I blinked, rubbing my eyes.

The room was empty!

I got up, searched the bath and the closet, and even peered behind the hangings. Had I seen a ghost? Near the bathroom door I seemed to see the print of a small, damp foot; but it might have been my own footprint, left after my bath. Finally, telling myself practically that I had had a vivid dream, I went back to bed. But it was hours before I slept.

Chapter
Three

It was a little after seven when I awoke, and pale brilliant arrows of light were gleaming through the curtains.

Carla knocked and came in on soft-slippered feet, bearing a laden tray, which she set invitingly near my bed.

"I've brought your breakfast, Miss Moore. I'm sorry no one thought to ask last night what you wanted for breakfast, but with Miss Deirdre running away again——" she broke off sharply and moved to the window, turning her face aside and drawing the curtains, so that a flood of sunlight filled the room. "Anyhow, Mr. Lowden told me to bring you up the same as Miss Deirdre's. Mrs. McLeod, she never wants anything but coffee, and Mr. Brant has had his breakfast and gone out long ago."

"It looks lovely. That was very kind of Mr. Lowden," I said, inspecting the heavy china coffee-pot; the covered dish, which proved to contain eggs and bacon and crisp, toasted muffins, dripping with butter, all hot and steaming fresh; and the slice of pale honeydew melon. I pulled a robe over my nightgown and poured myself a cup of coffee; then something Carla had said came back to me. "Miss Deirdre—does she run away often?" I asked.

"She never did before, Miss—not when Miss Fields was here. That was the other nurse. Now, sometimes——" she broke off again, clearly uneasy. "It's not my place to gossip about it, Miss Moore. You should hear it from Mr. Brant."

I remembered Ross Hunter's words yesterday afternoon; remembered the telephone call that had summoned the housekeeper away from my room. I wondered who had been caring for Deirdre since her other nurse had gone. Miss Fields, I remembered, had been the young companion-nurse they had engaged for Deirdre. Killed in an accident, Brant had said, about six months ago, and since then they had had two nurses for Deirdre, the first harsh and jailerlike, the second apparently dissatisfied with life on Sanctuary Island. And who had cared for the girl since then? Somehow I could not see Martine McLeod spending her days with a demented child given to tantrums or to running away. I found myself growing more curious about my patient. Carla was moving toward the door. She said, "Mr. Brant said, when you finish your breakfast, Miss, he'll take you to meet Miss Deirdre."

I ate slowly, sitting beside the window, looking down at the peaceful beach and the woodland below me. The water threw back the sunshine in a thousand bizarre colors; outside the casements the sound of birdsong made the air bright and soft. Far out on the water I saw a motorboat, so far away that it was just a black speck against the horizon. A man in a red plaid jacket went whistling down one of the paths. Ross Hunter? Here at this hour of the morning? I was getting entirely too curious about Ross Hunter, I decided.

I debated changing into uniform but finally decided against it. If a former nurse had been harsh with Deirdre, the sight of a white uniform might prejudice her mind against me. I knew nothing about the girl except what Brant and Martine had told me, and laymen, I had found, were prone either to exaggerate abnormal behavior or to underestimate it, thinking that if they ignored it, it would go away. One of the more pitiful cases in my early years as a nurse had been that of a mentally retarded child who at eight could neither speak clearly nor take himself to the toilet; his parents insisted that he was simply highstrung and that he had "a little speech defect." Not until he was fourteen did they yield to the inevitable and have have the hopeless little creature committed to an institution.

So I knew that I could not trust either Martine's denunciation of her daughter as "a crafty little liar" or Brant McLeod's insistence that she was "a sunny, happy child."

30

I should have insisted on talking to the doctor in charge of her case before meeting her, but this was no time to think of that. I drank the last of my coffee, showered quickly and brushed my teeth, and put on a blue-and-white-striped summer dress.

I found my way downstairs more easily this morning; as I stepped into the enormous hall, which seemed to need only a suit of armor or two to serve as the set for a Hollywood epic, Brant McLeod came out of the library. He looked up and saw me on the stairs, and for a moment he scowled as if trying to remember who I was and where the devil I had appeared from. The scowl made his face formidable, and I found myself hoping he would never direct that scowl at me. Then his face cleared and he seemed to remember who I was. I had been classified in the appropriate pigeonhole, the proper category and relationship to Brant McLeod: "nurse, one, psychiatric, for the stepsister of."

"Miss Moore," he said, and I stifled a tendency to click my heels and salute. But he only sighed. "I suppose I may as well take you up to Deirdre."

"I would like to know a bit more about her, Mr. McLeod. Does she have the freedom of the house? Of her room? Of the grounds? Exactly what—"

"Use your own discretion about that," he interrupted curtly; "you're the nurse. Give her as much freedom as you think is safe. As I said last night, we'd rather she'd think of you as a friend—not a nurse or, God forbid, a jailer. Treat her as if she were sick."

"But she *is* sick, isn't she?"

"Oh, yes," he said wearily, "she's sick, all right. But use your own judgment."

This was incredible. I said in my stiffest professional manner, "Mr. McLeod, if I am to be responsible for the safety and well-being of my patient, I really must know the limits of my responsibility. If you are unwilling to talk about my patient"—I repeated the word patient deliberately—"I must insist on a conference with the physician in charge of the case."

He stood back, blinking slightly, and his grim face trem-

31

bled with the shadow, only the shadow, of a smile. "You *do* sound formidable. I guess you really are a nurse. I'd almost forgotten. You don't look the part."

Still very much on my professional dignity, I snapped, "Would you care to see my credentials, Mr. McLeod? Or I can change into uniform if you would rather."

"Good Lord, no," he exclaimed. "No offense meant, Miss Moore, and for God's sake don't feel you must wear uniforms; we'd much rather you didn't, and I'm sure Deirdre would rather! But—I had a picture of a psychiatric nurse and you don't fit it." He gestured. "Somebody built like a battleship—not a pocket-sized blond."

"Someone capable, in short, of handling a disturbed or violent patient? Please, Mr. McLeod, don't be misled," I said, somewhat ruffled; "pocket-sized I may be, and blond I may be, but I've had plenty of training in handling disturbed patients, including adult men in acute mania. Is Deirdre likely to become violent at short notice, then? You see why I must ask these questions."

Now he looked both angry and agitated. "Violent? Deirdre? God forbid! I beg of you, don't think of my sister as a raving lunatic!"

"Well, what *is* she?"

I must have sounded as exasperated as I felt, for he said, "Meet her first; that's all I ask. Just meet her."

He started past me, up the stairs. "I should have come upstairs," he said. "There was no point in making you come down; her room is right next to yours." He climbed silently, his tread firm on the carpeted stairs.

"Carla told me that your sister ran away yesterday afternoon. Is she given to running away very often, then?"

He muttered, "I'll send that girl packing if she can't learn to hold her tongue"; then his mouth shut like an oyster shell, stubborn and firm. I started to explode, then held my temper, with great effort. Very well; I'd play it his way —for the moment. But there would be a showdown one of these days. Mr. Brant McLeod might be fond of this demented stepsister of his, but it seemed to be his only virtue. He was, I decided, quite the rudest and most arrogant man I'd ever know.

The halls were incredible; even though the first shock

32

of living in what seemed like a Hollywood set was beginning to wear off, I was quite certain I'd never really get used to it. We passed my door, which was slightly ajar, and within I heard the soft whine of a vacuum cleaner. Nearby was a paneled door; Brant pushed it open and stood back for me to precede him. A flood of sunlight poured from inside, and I stepped into the first light or cheerful room I had seen in the Castle.

The light came from a wide bay window with pointed arches, the sunlight reflecting on white walls and thin blue hangings. The light was fretted and strangely patterned; in one quick glance I saw that the windows were reinforced by ornamental grilles which looked more modern than their stone casements. It was a moment before I realized that their delicate lacework was steel-strong and that, effectively, the antique windows were barred! It was enough of a shock to stop me still.

Brant came in behind me, closing the door. I looked quickly around the room. In the bay window, a card table was drawn up. Although her back was to the door, I recognized the gray bun of Mrs. Meadows, the housekeeper; and facing me, her face bent over a checkerboard, was a slight fair-haired girl in a pink dress. She had been so absorbed in the game that she had not heard the door; she reached out, suddenly, and jumped one of the men, removing it from the board with a little squeak.

"Winning your game, Deedee?" I hardly recognized Brant McLeod's voice; it was gentle, even tender.

The girl looked up. She saw me, and with a little jump, she rose to her feet and shrank back, gathering herself together as if for flight. Mrs. Meadows rose quickly, turning in agitation, and the girl stood silent, her eyes fixed on me. They were enormous eyes, huge and silver-gray and framed in dark feathery lashes; eyes too large for her little, heart-shaped face, which was rosy-pale, with beautifully shaped, small, regular features and a dimpled mouth. The strangest thing was that in the beauty of the childish face I could see the features of Martine McLeod; but Martine's face was all strength, and this face was shy and shrinking —and scared.

Deirdre whispered, "Who is *she?*"

33

Brant said gently, "This is Susan Moore, dear. She's going to look after you and keep you company for a while, if you like having her around."

I was observing the girl closely. The pink dress was beautifully tidy and well fitted and well cut. She was clean as a cat, her hands well kept except for the telltale bitten fingernails that betrayed so many otherwise-normal children. Her hair was combed, clean, silky-straight, cut square around her small chin. Obviously, then, she was not completely intractable—she could be fed, dressed, washed and kept clean. She could talk, and presumably, she could understand what was said to her.

I looked at the checker game; the move she had made showed intelligence—not that I was an expert on checkers, but at least she wasn't an idiot. I couldn't help feeling a good deal of relief. For the mentally sick man, woman, or child there is always some hope—a ray of hope, at least. If the mind is there, some way to reach it may be found. But I have never been able to face the tragedy of the idiot, the imbecile, the defective, hopelessly imprisoned in a vegetablelike existence.

I should have known. Any reasonably skilled practical nurse can handle an idiot. They would not have been so anxious to have a competent, companionable professional for a girl living a vegetable life.

I smiled, as ingratiatingly as possible, at Deirdre. I said, "Hello, Deirdre. I see you've been playing checkers."

"Obviously, you have good eyesight," the girl retorted, and I was startled almost into silence. So it wasn't defective intelligence, then, at all; this child was shrewd and even witty. She was not looking quite so scared now. She looked me up and down. "You're a nurse, aren't you?"

I thought swiftly about that. Brant preferred me not to act like one; yet if this girl were really as shrewd as her first remarks indicated, I had better not start off by lying to her. When dealing with the insane, it can be just as dangerous to underestimate as to overestimate them.

I said quietly, "I have a registered nurse's degree, yes."

"So you're my new keeper?" She smiled a little lopsided smile.

Lightning-swift, I answered, "Whether I act like a

keeper or like a friend will depend on you and how you act."

It set her back on her heels. She blinked a little; she thought about it. Then, slowly, she smiled. The lovely little face was almost breathtaking when she smiled, and I could see why it was hard for Brant to accept that this exquisite child was not completely sane.

She said, "Well, at least you're honest about it. That last nurse kept trying to pretend we'd just be good little pals together."

Brant had stood in the background; now he said, "I have some work to attend to, Deedee, so I'll leave you and Miss Moore to get acquainted."

She went and wound her arms around his neck, standing on tiptoe, cajolingly, like a child half her age. "Will you come and take me swimming this afternoon?"

He hesitated. "If you're a good girl, yes; we'll show Miss Moore the beach."

"Perhaps you'd like to finish your game," I suggested.

Deirdre looked back at the checkerboard indifferently. "Oh, Mrs. Meadows is going to win this game," she said. "I'm not very good at checkers. It's a bore. But it's the only game we both know how to play."

"Then it's kind of her to play it with you," Brant said reprovingly. The housekeeper rose with dignity.

Deirdre turned to her and said, with a melting sweetness, "I'm sorry. It *is* nice of you to play with me, and I'm not bored with *you*, Mrs. Meadows."

"Thank you, Miss Deirdre," said the old woman, unruffled. "Perhaps Miss Moore will know some games you'll like better. Be a good girl, now, and I'll leave you to yourselves." She left the room, and I was alone with Deirdre McLeod.

Deirdre stood looking at the closed door for a moment. "She thinks I'm crazy," she said at last. "Do *you* think I'm crazy?"

Here I was on more or less familiar ground. No one is more certain of his own sanity than the lunatic, and there is nothing more futile than discussing it. Of course, we are never allowed to use those words in mental hospitals any more—no one is "crazy," "insane," or even, nowadays, "mentally ill." But I had had good results, so far, with Deirdre, with the blunt truth.

"How do I know whether you are or not?" I asked. "I don't know you yet."

Unorthodox, perhaps; perhaps I should have used some vague generalities. But Deirdre brightened and she smiled.

"What's your name?"

"Susan Moore."

"Can I call you Susan?"

"If you want to," I replied carelessly, "unless you think we should call each other Miss Moore and Miss McLeod."

Her face, mobile and sweet, suddenly darkened like a visible shadow. "My name isn't McLeod," she said sulkily; "I'm Deirdre Adrienne Clereau."

Yes; Brant had spoken of the girl as his stepsister, Martine's daughter by a prior marriage. They were actually no relation, then—for all his solicitude. Deirdre was still staring belligerently at me, and I said quietly, "I'd forgotten. Mr. McLeod speaks of you as his sister; perhaps that's why."

I was taking stock of the room, which was bright and prettily furnished; beyond it an open door led into a small bedroom in blue and white and a tiled bath. On the shelves were books. Rather at a loss as to what to say or do next, I went and examined them. Most of them were children's classics; *Robin Hood, The Wind in the Willows, The Hobbit.* There were one or two sea stories, but it looked more like a child's library than a young girl's. I decided to wait and observe her awhile before trying to estimate her mental age or intelligence.

"Do you like to read?" I asked.

She shrugged rather listlessly. "Some. I'm getting bored with those books. Brant reads everything before he lets me have it. I'm not allowed to read newspapers or most of the books in the library."

I began to wonder how I could divert and amuse this girl. Did she do lessons? Did they expect her to spend her days shut up in these rooms reading children's books and playing children's games? "What do you like to do best?"

"I like swimming," she answered eagerly, "and bird-watching, though I can't do much on this side of the island. May I show you my bird charts? Brant got me a pair of good binoculars and I have a feeding tray—there were a pair of orioles there this morning."

I allowed her to bring her bird charts and noted that they were neatly kept, though the handwriting was childish and sprawling. She brought out some picture books of birds and chattered with animation, and before long she was sitting on the arm of my chair showing me the pictures and telling me about the birds of the island. We were both surprised by the arrival of Carla with trays for lunch, which we ate at the table by the window. By this time I was beginning to realize that Deirdre was—most of the time, probably—tractable and intelligent, if childish for her age. Brant McLeod had suggested that I allow her as much freedom as I felt was safe. Evidently she was allowed to walk near the house on her bird-watching expeditions. I considered suggesting a walk, but before I could mention it, Brant arrived, walking into the room without knocking.

"Ready for a swim, Deedee?" he asked.

Her eyes shone with anticipation, and she jumped up and ran into the bedroom. I followed, to find her turning over a pair of swimsuits hanging on the bathroom door. She said impatiently, "I can get myself dressed and undressed! Why don't you go and get ready yourself?"

I glanced around the bedroom quickly, with a trained nurse's eye. I noticed that her dressing table contained no glass bottles or even nail files or scissors. There were only a hairbrush and comb and a box of talcum powder. The bathroom was equally bare of anything potentially dangerous. Evidently her former nurse had considered it necessary to take at least these precautions—and I knew myself, by experience, how quickly even the mildest-seeming disturbed person could turn violent. I said, ignoring the angry flush on her face, "I think I'd prefer to stay with you while you dress, if you don't mind."

"But I do mind!" she flared at me.

A showdown already? Or was she merely exploring

how far she could go in defying me? I said calmly, "I'm very sorry that it bothers you to have me here," and I firmly took a seat in a blue-chintz rocker.

Her face flushed; she said ungraciously, "*I* don't care," and without a further glance at me she pulled off her pink dress. I noticed that she hung it neatly on a hanger, though she allowed her pink cotton panties and white slip to lie where they fell. She wriggled into the bottom of a brief green bathing suit and struggled with the hooks at the back of its halter top.

I said, "May I help you hook it?"

"I can manage—oh, go ahead; you're here, you may as well make yourself useful," she said rudely. I got up and came over to her, brushing aside her flaxen hair to hook the halter. She turned around. The suit, I supposed, was at least a 32; her body was the firm, small, maturing body of a sixteen-year-old, but the suit gave her, somehow, the sexless look of a little girl. Or was it simply the Alice-in-Wonderland hairdo or her wide, childish eyes?

She said, "You're coming in swimming, aren't you? You can swim, can't you?"

I could, and I supposed that I should be ready to swim, since my patient, if whimsical and unpredictable, might suddenly do something dangerous. We returned to the outer room, and Brant McLeod, taking in the situation at a glance, said, "Go and get changed, Miss Moore. I'll walk down to the beach with Deedee, and you can join us there as soon as you're ready."

I stepped to the door of Deirdre's room and stopped in confusion, not certain of the way to my own apartment. Deirdre pointed and said, "Right around that corner."

So close? I had, indeed, got turned around in the corridors of the castle. Dierdre winked suddenly at me.

"It's all done with mirrors," she said in a stage whisper, and she picked up Brant's hand loosely in her thin, cool fingers. "We'll see you at the beach. You *can* find your way down?" she asked. There was a surprising twinkle in her eyes.

"I think so," I answered, grinning back at her.

Back in my own room—where I noticed that the bed

38

had been made and the bathroom tidied—and even the Kleenex I had used this morning emptied from the waste-basket—I quickly climbed into my plain black bathing suit. I pulled a pink terrycloth robe over it, put a bathing cap into my pocket, and started down the stairs. A maid in a dark uniform and apron was sweeping the stairs and looked up at me curiously and, I thought, enviously. True enough, I was out for a swim in the sunlight —and yet I was just as much of an employee as she was. Maybe more so, since it seemed I'd be tied down night and day to the whims of a willful and unpredictable child.

On the second landing I suddenly heard racing footsteps, and a small-sized cyclone tore around the corner, yapping, and tried to climb up my legs, licking my sandaled feet; whereupon a smaller whirlwind dashed around the landing, scooping up what now appeared to be a very large Newfoundland dog. Then the smaller apparition straightened up, revealing itself as a very slight boy with straight, dark hair in an English pudding-basin haircut. He wore damp swim trunks and espadrilles and nothing else. He looked up at me with wide blue eyes, eyes disturbingly like Deirdre's, and at odds with his dark face. With both hands on the enormous dog's collar, he struggled to control it as it rolled over and over, slobbering at his bare toes with its huge tongue.

"I'm sorry bout Thumbelina," he said in a childish but extremely mannerly voice; "she's a little exuberant."

What an odd, precocious little boy! And—*Thumbelina!* I looked at the monstrous rug-hound, remembering the original of that name, who could curl up inside a buttercup, and chuckled. "I should think *Jumbo* would be a better name for—er—Thumbelina," I commented, "but it's quite all right; I like dogs." I patted Thumbelina's shaggy mane, and the resultant ecstasies made the entire staircase vibrate.

He was looking up at me curiously, over the big dog. "I don't know you. You're not any of the maids."

"My name is Susan Moore," I told him. "I'm a nurse. Who are you?"

"I'm Jeremy Duncan McLeod, Miss Moore," he said

politely. Then small-boy curiosity broke through the façade of manners again. "Are you Deirdre's new nurse?"

"Yes, I am."

His small face suddenly twitched and twisted. "Why does she need a nurse? She isn't sick," he demanded furiously, "and why won't they ever let me see her any more? Why won't they even let me *swim* with her any more?" I could see that he was struggling with tears. "She can't be sick or she'd be in bed, and she's out swimming with Brant, and Thumbie and I were swimming, and Brant made me go in, and Deedee called to me, and Brant wouldn't let me speak to her, and she *cried!*" He wiped his eyes, furiously, with water-wrinkled small fists. "Why can't I even speak to *my own sister* any more?"

So this was Martine's younger child by old Mr. Mc-Leod; Deirdre's and Brant's little half-brother. I didn't know what to say to him. What could I say? I said, "Sometimes people don't look sick when they are, Jeremy."

"Well, if it was anything catching like the measles, she'd be in bed," he argued angrily, "and Brant wouldn't be around her either." He bent, and I could see that he was struggling with tears, which he hid by hiding his flushed face in Thumbelina's huge, rough coat. "I *used* to be with Deedee all the time. Even when she was sicker than she is, and couldn't talk. Miss Margo used to let me come in every night and have supper with Deedee, and I used to swim with her and play on the beach! Why can't I even play with my own sister any more?"

My heart ached for the child; but all I could say was, gently, "You'd better ask your mother and father, Jeremy."

His face took on a bitter, almost cynical expression, too wise for his years—I supposed he was nine or ten. "Huh! You think *they'd* tell me anything?"

A shout of "Jerry! " came from the foot of the staircase, and a sturdy young woman in a frumpish bathing suit and robe trudged up the stairs toward us. "Here, you little dickens, where 'ave you got to—oh, excuse me, Miss," she said, breaking off as she saw me. "Master Jeremy, where are your manners? And take that great beast off to the playroom, do!"

"Yes'm," he muttered, and, tugging at Thumbelina's collar, ducking his head to hide his tear-smudged face, he dashed up the stairs. The young woman gazed after him, and her face, plain as a pudding but good-humored, with sandy freckles splotched on her nose, was filled with more kindliness and tolerance than her rather sharp words would allow. "Eh, dear, that great animal, I hope the beastie didn't hurt you, Miss. You'll be Miss Deirdre's new nurse?"

"I'm Susan Moore."

"Pleased to meet you, Nurse," she said formally.

"And you are . . . ?"

"I'm Hester Cairncross, Nurse: I'm here to look after little Master Jerry, and a handful he can be, too. Especially now." She gave me a sidelong look I was beginning to recognize.

"You're not American?"

"Scottish, Miss. From Edinburgh." She pronounced it "Edinbro." "He goes to school on the mainland, winters, but in this great house someone has to look after the wee boy, and *that* one . . ." she gave an eloquent little jerk of her head. "Sometimes I thank the good Lord, Miss, that I wasn't born with a silver spoon in my mouth. That one doesn't care if her bairns so much as get their suppers or say their prayers before they go to bed! I shouldn't say so, Miss, it's not my place, but since poor Miss Margo died, those poor children have been less looked after than if their mother was a charwoman!"

I would have liked to listen more to the voluble Hester —I felt I might learn much from her—but I realized that time was passing, and my charge was being left on Brant's hands. I said, "I must get out and look after Deirdre. I hope we'll be good friends."

"Indeed, we should be," she said forthrightly, "and I must see that he's not brought the great dog into his bedroom again. I'll see ye later, Miss." She tramped heavily off up the stairs, while I sped downward, aware that I had been neglecting my own charge.

But they seemed not to have missed me. I found Deirdre and Brant on the beach, Deirdre tucking her long fair hair into a bathing cap. In swimming trunks, his

41

smooth body bronzed, the sullen arrogance vanished from his face, Brant looked younger and carefree. He actually smiled as I dropped my robe to the sand; then he turned to Deirdre.

"Now remember, Deedee," he said; "you stay inside the markers"—he pointed to them—"while you're swimming, and mind you don't let her get too chilled, Miss Moore." Then his face suddenly lightened in a grin. "But I needn't remind a registered nurse of that, I suppose." And there was no sarcasm in the comment.

"*You* swim out with me," Deirdre coaxed, and Brant laughed, took her hand, and raced with her into the shallow, lapping waves. I felt my way out carefully, but the sand was smooth, and the descent gradual, with no sudden drop into deep water. When the water reached my waist, I lowered myself and swam out to join the other swimmers.

Deirdre, her pixie face flushed beneath her green bathing cap, smiled at me as she turned on her back to float. "Oh, it's *heavenly* out here! I could swim *all day!*"

"Who taught you to swim?"

Her face shadowed again and she said, "I don't remember—"

Brant cut in swiftly, "I believe Deedee learned to swim about as soon as she could walk."

I found Deirdre an expert swimmer, and she carefully kept inside the floats that marked the limits of the beach. "There are sharp underwater reefs beyond them," Brant warned me, "and a dangerous riptide. You seem to be a good, strong swimmer, but whatever you do, don't try to do anything foolish like swimming around the island. There's an undertow and a bad current, and sharp rocks—and you could be swept onto them and smashed. And of course you watch Deedee carefully whenever she's in the water." He spoke in an undertone, but she looked round at us with that sharp, shrewd little smile which was the only hint of Martine I could see in her face.

When we were tired of swimming we went back to the shore. Deirdre played childishly with the fine sand, letting it sift through her fingers and digging holes for the sea to fill. She seemed trustworthy enough on the beach, but I never took my eyes from her. I took advantage of a moment when she was preoccupied with smoothing the top of what seemed to be a sand-castle to say in a low voice to Brant, "Two things, Mr. McLeod. First of all, may I ask you not to discuss Deirdre in her presence? I'm sure she understands everything you say, and it troubles her. Second, I met her brother on the stairs—"

His face clouded. "Poor little Jerry. Poor little devil; he can't understand it."

"Is it really necessary to keep the children apart? He misses her, and as far as I can tell, Deirdre appears to be trustworthy most of the time."

"Martine ordered it," he said, and looked away again.

"But I understand Miss Fields used to allow them to be together a good deal—"

"That has nothing to do with it," he said, rising abruptly, "and I prefer not to discuss it, Miss Moore." He turned to Deirdre, who had abandoned her sand castle and was coming toward us. She had pulled off her bathing cap, and her flaxen hair surrounded her in a nimbus of light. The wet suit cling to her childish body smoothly. If Martine did not care for her daughter, at least she dressed her exquisitely.

She was looking toward the edge of the beach, where a small group of tiny seabirds were feeding. I asked, "Are those sandpipers, Deirdre?"

"Yes, they are. I suppose you know the gulls"—she pointed overhead—"but we get some land birds on the island, too, of course; we're close enough to the mainland and we have so much woodland."

"I understand it's a Government bird sanctuary," I said. "How much of the land actually belongs to you, Mr. McLeod, and must we keep out of the bird sanctuary?"

"Good Lord, no," Brant said, "as long as you don't disturb the birds' nests or their eggs or anything. Actually we own only this little strip of beach and about fifteen acres of woodland behind the house. But feel free to explore the whole island. If you like birds, the place should suit you to a T."

"I don't know much about them," I said, smiling at Deirdre, "but perhaps she can teach me."

"Oh, yes; I'd like to."

Brant took Deirdre's hand. "What about it? Shall we take Miss Moore on a walk around the island?"

"All right. Come on, Susan!" She stretched her free hand to me, and I felt a curious warmth as the small, cold fingers closed trustingly around mine. She seemed so childlike that it was hard to realize that out in the world this girl would be wearing high heels, rolling her hair nightly in curlers, idolizing the latest teen-age film star, and chattering about dates and boy friends and the top ten rock 'n' roll records. Or would she?

She chatted cheerily about birds as we walked along the beach. A small flight of sandpipers fluttered away, and she pointed gravely to the jellylike remnants of their feast. "Be careful of those things. They look pretty but they hurt something awful if you step on them with bare feet," she warned me. I had seen Portuguese men-of-war before, but I did not tell her so, thanking her for the warning.

At the edge of the beach a steep path led upward and we walked for some time under low-hanging trees, fragrant and pungent with loose grayish bark. The path was cool and Deirdre, tossing her fair hair, looked like a dryad in her green suit. Brant moved more slowly, seeming preoccupied and weighed down. He was watching Deirdre carefully and I wondered why.

The woodland path ended suddenly, and we came out at the top of a sharp downward slope. Before us lay a broad, rocky expanse of beach, behind which cliffs and caves rose. Sea caves! It was a wild, romantic place; yet Brant, who had arrived there first, surveyed it gloomily, turning to wait for Deirdre. He was biting his lip and I saw him, despite the cool path, wipe sudden beads of sweat from his forehead. Deirdre, who had lagged behind us to peer at a nest high in one of the trees, suddenly came out at the top of the rocky slope.

She stopped dead in her tracks. Her fair face paled, turning bone white, and her small hand flew to her mouth. She bit her fingers. She whispered, "Not—not *here!*"

Brant wet his dry lips with his tongue. He said, "I thought we might show Susan the sea caves, old girl. And we might find some more pretty shells for your room."

"No! No! I won't go down there!" Her voice rose suddenly, high and excited, almost to a scream. She was suddenly shaking like a leaf.

As I stepped toward her to take her hand, Brant said sharply, "Oh, come on, Deedee; such nonsense! There's nothing to hurt you there—"

"No! *No!*" It was a piercing, eerie scream. She wrapped her arms suddenly around the bole of a tree and shrieked, "I won't go down there! I won't! Please, please, don't make me, don't—"

I moved quickly between them. With a curt, almost harsh gesture, I said, "Quiet, Mr. McLeod."

He opened his mouth in indignation, then shut it again.

I took Deirdre's cold hand in mine and said, "Nobody is going to make you go down there if you don't want to."

"I—won't go down there," she whispered, and began to cry, suddenly throwing her arms around me. "Oh, Susan, Susan, can't I go back to the other beach?"

"Miss Moore, if you humor her—"

I gave him a look that, if it had been fire, would have left him a very small and wrinkled cinder and said, "Not a word, if you please." I turned my attention back to the trembling, pitifully small little figure in my arms, soothing her gently. "Of course you can go back to the other beach. Come on, dear. It's all right. Don't cry."

She gave me a scared, hesitant, hopeful look. I urged her gently back toward the woodland path. She took a step, then another, clinging hard to my hand, her face turned awkwardly away from the rocky downward slope. Her steps were stiff and awkward, as if she moved through water; but when the shadow of the woods had folded around us again I heard her sigh, a long, trembling sound, and her steps seemed to loosen and move more freely. By the time we came out into the sunlight of the other beach, she was breathing naturally, the last trace of sobs gone. Shaking out her shining hair, she danced down toward the remnants of her sand castle, which had been lapped away by the incoming tide. She splashed it gleefully. "All gone," she cried. "Well, I can build another one tomorrow."

I looked up at the lowering sun. Far out on the sea a

blue haze moved, and I felt that a cold sea fog would soon be moving inland. Hesitantly, trying my authority for the first time, I said, "I suppose we had better go inside, Deirdre. It's getting cold."

She picked up her robe docilely and followed me up the path. I let her walk ahead. Brant, gazing grimly after me, gestured to me to wait.

"Well," he said, "you've seen her in action."

I looked at him in amazement. "Did you force her up there simply so that she would—you *knew* what her reaction would be?"

"I wanted you to see," he said stubbornly.

Well, I had seen. But my opinion of Brant McLeod slipped another notch. "You—you *sadist!*" I exploded; *I* turned my back on him and followed my charge to the castle and up into her rooms.

Chapter
Four

THE DAYS on Sanctuary Island soon fell into a routine that was, if monotonous, not unpleasant. Deirdre and I breakfasted together in her rooms and spent the mornings in walking about the island and bird-watching or in playing various childish games. I found her shrewd enough, in spite of her childishness, and since I was careful to avoid the rocky beach with the sea caves at the far side of the island, I found her docile and tractable. In the afternoons we usually went swimming. Brant joined us once or twice, but he spent his time, after the briefest and most formal of polite greetings, entirely with Deirdre.

I had had no further conversation with either of the older generation of the McLeods, although once, from an upper window, I had seen Lowden wheeling old Mr. Alexander down one of the elaborately landscaped walks in the back garden; and two or three times in the hallway I encountered Martine McLeod. It struck me as somewhat strange that Martine never asked about her daughter or visited her in her rooms: but if this seemed strange, it was stranger still that Deirdre never asked about her mother or even mentioned her name, far less inquired why she was ignored.

Had Martine simply abandoned her daughter, emotionally, after discovering that the girl would not be a credit to her? It would have been easier if I had known the history of the case or could have consulted Deirdre's doctor. As far as I could tell, they were making no effort whatever to help the girl, and that was almost incredible. Deirdre was neither violent nor ineducable. A special school, perhaps, with psychotherapy and special training, might help her to recover and lead something like a normal life.

47

Why were they content simply to have a resident custodian? It certainly wasn't a question of money—not if Duncarlie Castle's style of living was any indication—and for very little more than my salary, they could have had her in a good private sanitarium receiving specialized, individual psychotherapy.

Did they *want* her to recover? If so, why were they doing nothing?

I had been a week on Sanctuary Island when the telephone in my room rang late one night. Deirdre had been tucked in bed, and I had seen her asleep. Retiring to my own room with a book from the library, I realized that there was really little else to do here. The servants had shown no inclination to talk to me, and in any case I could not, it seemed, mix with them openly without losing face. From my window, looking down at the landing, I saw a boat at the pier and Martine, beautifully dressed, being handed on board by Brant, who got in beside her. I recognized, at the tiller of the boat, the old man who had brought me to Sanctuary Island. Brant was in evening clothes, and I found myself wondering where they were going—and why old Mr. McLeod was not with them.

Were they going to a concert or to a party on the mainland? Martine's beautiful gown, cut low on her shoulders and sweeping back, looked more suitable for an evening at the opera than for a vacation world where most of the islanders I had seen wore swim trunks day in and day out. I realized, not without amusement, that I was jealous. And furthermore, I was being a cat. Why shouldn't Brant escort his young stepmother to some entertainment where his father, aging and an invalid, found it impossible to go? Old Mr. Alexander, I had heard, never left the island now. And if Martine were Brant's own mother I wouldn't give it a second thought.

But Martine is nearer to Brant's own age, I thought, and then was shocked at myself. I was worse than any small-town gossip. I pulled down the window shade with a slam and heard behind me a small startled sound. I whirled to see Deirdre in her nightgown standing behind me.

"Deirdre! What are you doing here?" I said severely. "You are supposed to be in bed."

48

She made no answer, staring fixedly at the lowered window shade, and again I saw, as if printed there, the picture of Brant bent over Martine with gentle precaution, handing her into the boat.

This was familiar ground enough. The child, deprived of her mother's natural affection and care, had evidently formed a typical adolescent's jealous attachment to her stepbrother—and who could blame her? Brant was the only soul on the island who seemed to pay the slightest attention to the poor child!

Deirdre said, staring at the window, "Where are *they* going?"

"I don't know," I said; "perhaps to a party or a concert."

"Why does *he* have to take her?"

Since I had just been wondering that myself, I could hardly reprove the girl. I said, "In any case, you should be in bed. And how did you get in here anyway?" I demanded, realizing that I had not heard my door open and close. The girl must be able to move as softly as a cat!

She only giggled, and I wondered disquietingly if I should lock her in her room at night. If she were going to start wandering around the house at night . . . I said, "Back to bed this minute, young lady," and I rose to accompany her back to her own room. She went quietly, without protest, but her small mouth was fixed and sullen.

"Now will you stay in bed, or must I lock you in?" I asked, recalling that a direct appeal to her reason frequently worked better than subterfuge.

"It wouldn't do you any good to lock me in," she said, with that sudden shrewd, sly look that was her only rare sign of abnormality. Then she smiled her usual small, sweet pixie smile and said, "But I'll stay here. Where would I go, anyhow?"

Where, indeed? But how did I know what mischief my charge might work? I decided to demand an interview with her mother very soon; I literally could not watch the girl twenty-four hours a day, and if she were to be subject to these sudden unpredictable impulses to wander or to run away, I must be given authority to lock her in. This whole affair was baffling, anyhow. I tucked her into bed,

49

turned out the light, and left her again, not without a feeling of disquiet.

I finally decided to leave the door into the hall slightly ajar, hoping that I would hear Deirdre if she decided on another nighttime ramble. I had lost interest in my book and sat frowning at the window. I'd at least make sure she was sound asleep before going to bed myself.

Then the telephone rang, and I picked up the receiver. "Hello?"

Lowden's voice, speaking on the house telephone, said, "An outside call for you, Miss Moore," and I heard a click.

"Hello. Is that Susan Moore?"

"Yes," I said, not recognizing the voice and wondering who on earth would be calling me here; "who is it, please?"

"This is Ross Hunter," the man said. "Remember me? You met me the first day we came to the island."

"Mr. Hunter, of course."

"I'm sorry to call so late," he said, "but I thought you might be tied up with the kid. She keeping you on your toes?"

"Yes, I've been pretty busy," I admitted, and he chuckled.

"I suppose, though, that you do get some time off?"

When my salary had been arranged, it had been indicated that I would receive occasional afternoons off; but this had not yet been discussed. I said so, and Ross Hunter said, "Trust Martine for that. Well, look; do you suppose you could get away tomorrow afternoon or the next day?"

"I could try," I said cautiously; "why?"

"I don't suppose you've seen all the island yet from the water, and it's a beautiful trip. I thought you might like to see it from my speedboat."

The thought was intriguing. Ross Hunter seemed pleasantly normal after the tense family atmosphere of Duncarlie Castle, and it would be pleasant to have an afternoon free. I said, "I'll ask and let you know, Mr. Hunter. It sounds wonderful."

"It would be even more wonderful if I could persuade you to make that Ross—Susan," he said, and I smiled and repeated, "Ross."

When I had hung up the receiver, I lay back, hands

50

tucked behind my head, smiling. An odd little surge of happiness suddenly bubbled up in me. For the first time since I had first seen Raymond Grantham, I felt free and happy, free and pleased at another man's attentions. I told myself sensibly not to lose my head; after all, Ross Hunter was the first presentable male who had shown me any interest—I could hardly count Old Jim or Lowden as accessible men!

And Brant McLeod?

I laughed at my own mental question as I put out the light. That arrogant, ill-mannered brute! No wonder he had to fall back on the company of his own stepmother!

The next morning, leaving Deirdre over her breakfast, I went downstairs and knocked at the door of the dining room. Brant was there, bent over a stack of letters and a folded newspaper, while at the end of the table old Mr. Alexander was eating bacon and fried cakes in silence. He looked up as I came in, and he frowned slightly as if he could not remember quite who I was.

I apologized for my intrusion. "I wanted to speak to Mrs. McLeod," I told them, and old Mr. Alexander, raising his grizzled head, said, "Martine won't be down before noon; never is. What can I do for you?"

"I was wondering if I might have an afternoon off this week," I said, "but certainly I can discuss that with Mrs. McLeod later."

Brant raised his head. "Haven't you been given regular time off?"

"No, Mr. McLeod. I was told that it would be arranged."

"Well, if you have anything you want to do this afternoon, we can certainly arrange it," Brant said curtly. "I'll talk to Martine about it, and after this we'll see that you have some regular time of your own. I suppose Mrs. Meadows can look after Deedee, or if all else fails I can take her swimming."

"It's kind of you to take that much trouble," I said formally, "but there were other matters I wanted to discuss with Mrs. McLeod. She's the child's mother, after all."

Old Mr. Alexander said, "There shouldn't be anything to discuss. I won't have Martine worried about it. We've had enough trouble—"

51

"I'll handle it, Father," Brant said, rising quickly and shepherding me out of the room by skillfully getting between me and the old gentleman.

Out in the hall, Brant frowned at me and said, "Father doesn't like talking about Deirdre, as you ought to know. What do you think we engaged you for? If it's clothes, toys, books the girl needs, get them for her—Lowden or Mrs. Meadows will tell you what stores on the mainland handle our charge accounts, and how to order the things necessary. What else could it be?"

I said, "Mr. McLeod, no one here seems quite to understand the situation I am up against. In the first place, that girl should really be in a sanitarium. . . ."

I never saw a man's face change so quickly. He almost shoved me, by force, into his study and shut the door; then he turned to me with a quick, almost tigerish fierceness. "What do you mean? Has she shown any signs of violence? Has she—oh, God, has she attacked you?"

"No," I said, bewildered; "please calm down, Mr. McLeod. I only meant that custodial care such as you would give a—a mentally retarded child is hardly enough for Deirdre. If she were given psychotherapy, natural companionship, training—she might even recover enough to live a normal life. I have seen much worse cases make recoveries."

"You have observed her for one week," he said tersely, "and you make this diagnosis offhand, like this?"

I said, stiffly, "I've had no opportunity to talk with any doctor or psychotherapist who has examined her."

"Nor will you," he retorted. The set of his chin was suddenly brutal. "Take my word for it; we've gone everywhere and done everything. Deirdre is getting along very well as she is, and nothing would be accomplished by letting the doctors probe at her and shock her and lock her up. Here, she's free and happy, at least. I don't intend to discuss it any more; you accepted the position on these terms, and these terms are all you will be given."

"One would think," I said harshly, "that you didn't want Deirdre to get well."

His face softened. "Believe me, if I thought there was the faintest chance of that . . . but until you have had

52

more time, won't you please believe that we've exhausted all the possible resources? There's"—he swallowed suddenly and seemed to have trouble speaking—"nothing else we can do. Miss Moore, won't you sit down? I can't talk with you standing over me like an avenging angel." He sank into his desk chair and mopped his forehead, and I took a seat, bewildered. "Please believe me," he said.

"You make my position very difficult," I retorted. "In the first place, in a sanitarium she could be watched night and day. Since she seems given to running away, she can very easily escape my eyes."

"You could try locking her in," Brant said, "though I wish it weren't necessary. Or—I don't suppose you could manage to give her something that would keep her asleep all night?"

"Not without strict medical supervision," I said, scandalized.

He sighed. "I was afraid not. But isn't she usually trustworthy?"

"Usually . . ." I admitted.

"Then won't you do the best you can?" He looked harried, but he forced a smile, and somehow the smile hurt. It was strange to hear a note almost of pleading in the arrogant voice. "You can't imagine how hard it's been to find someone to take care of her—someone who won't treat her like a jailer, or else some flighty, irresponsible girl who'll want to be running off all the time. Can't you see that she needs someone like you?"

"Yes," I admitted slowly, aware that I was breaking the nurse's cardinal rule: *Don't get involved.* But Deirdre had touched my sympathies, and I would have hated to abandon her. And Brant had known her for years. If the case was really hopeless, perhaps the girl was happier on the island than under restraint in some asylum, being used perhaps to test unproved new drugs or treatments in the hope that they might do some good. Here, at least, she had some freedom, toys and games at will, her family close at hand, her birds, and her swimming. I said slowly, "Well, for the present—"

"Good." He rose, relieved, pressing my hand. "Good girl! And if you want to go out today—let me see; I'll arrange for Mrs. Meadows to stay with Deirdre in the early afternoon, and I'll take her swimming afterward. Where are you going? Shopping on the mainland, I suppose? Or you just want a holiday? Old Jim will run you ashore."

"Oh, no." I explained, and the more familiar frown dropped over his face. "Ross, eh? I might have known."

I asked, rather stiffly, "Is there any objection?"

"Objection? Oh, no. It's your own business." He grinned sardonically, moving toward the door; the interview was over. "Just that I should have realized that a beautiful girl on the island would have Ross trying to add another scalp to his belt. But then"—he made me an ironical little bow—"I daresay a competent professional woman would consider a warning on that score to be an insult to her intelligence. I'm quite, quite sure you can take care of yourself. I wish you a pleasant afternoon, Miss Moore." I found myself out on the stairs, hardly knowing how I had got there.

Deirdre did not protest when I told her that Mrs. Meadows would take care of her that afternoon, and she brightened when I informed her that Brant had promised to take her swimming. She manifested no curiosity about my intended absence, and I marked down another sympton—lack of affect, or emotional response—to the mental list I had begun to keep on this puzzling girl. However, after lunch, I went to my room to change into slacks and a sweater, for Ross had warned me that it often got cold on the water. When I came back, Deirdre was waiting rather anxiously. Mrs. Meadows was there, but Deirdre was paying no attention to the older woman.

"Where are you going?" Deirdre asked.

"Just out for the afternoon."

"I want to go downstairs with you," she said stubbornly, and Mrs. Meadows shrugged, walking along behind us as we went down toward the side door where Ross had promised to meet me.

I saw him down at the boat and turned cheerfully to say good-bye to Deirdre. "I'll see you at supper, now. Be a good girl."

Suddenly she gripped both my hands with her small, cold ones. "Susan, Susan," she begged, "you *will* come back? You're not going to go away and leave me, not for always, like *she* did? Promise me to come back, promise you're not going away?"

Startled, I pressed her hands—gently, careful not to frighten this timid response. "Why, of course I'll come back, you silly girl; I'll be back for supper."

"*She* said she'd be back for supper," Deirdre half-whimpered, clinging to my hands, until Mrs. Meadows gently loosened her grasp.

"Come now, Miss Deirdre, there's nothing for you to worry about." She added, in a swift, fierce whisper to me, "I thought she'd forgotten poor Miss Margo. Drowned on the water she was, they say, Miss, and the little thing never getting over it."

I put my arm firmly around Deirdre's waist. At first she held herself stiffly like a strange cat; then she relaxed and leaned against me.

"Deirdre," I said, "if somebody promised you to come back, and didn't, it wasn't me. I'll be back. I promise."

"All right; you can go," she said suddenly. She sighed and released me, holding out her hand to Mrs. Meadows.

With considerable relief, I walked down to the boat dock. I hardly knew what to think. I was glad that Deirdre was growing to trust me and to be fond of me. But why had she been so disturbed? And she had never spoken before of her former nurse, who had met an accidental death. In fact, this was the first time I could remember that Deirdre had spoken of anything in the past! Was it a good sign—or bad?

"Now, now," Ross said, stepping up to my side; "what a frown! Can't you leave your problems behind you? The crazy kid giving you trouble?" He saw my expression and added quickly, "No shoptalk, eh? Against professional ethics? Okay, Susan, we'll forget all about it for the moment. This is my boat." He gestured toward a small, trim, bright speedboat, lying in the slip beside the boathouse. It was painted a bright blue with two white lines running around it amidships, and it bore the title: PHOENIX.

"Why *Phoenix?*" I asked, as I let him hand me into the center of the boat, sitting down carefully on the cushion.

He chuckled merrily, kneeling to face the starting rope

of the outboard motor. "I call her the *Phoenix* because that's the only rare bird I never have any hope of seeing— here or anywhere else!" he said.

Today he wore a thick blue sweatshirt, with a hood that was flung back from his tanned face, and old, easy-fitting blue jeans spattered with white paint. He looked me over approvingly, and I was pleasantly conscious of the fit of my own sweater and tapered pants. "At least you don't think you have to wear high heels and a silk print for a boat ride," he commented, and gave the rope a quick tug. The outboard motor roared into life, drowning conversation, as we swung out and away from the dock. As we pulled away, Castle Duncarlie loomed briefly over us, then was cut off by the woodland between. Ross searched briefly in a locker beneath the seat and took out a pair of binoculars.

"You might like to look through these," he shouted; "there are other islands. I thought I'd give you a quick spin around some of the prettier ones, then come back to Sanctuary and show you my side of it."

We hardly spoke for the next hour, and it seemed that the tense and morbid atmosphere of Duncarlie Castle dissolved in the bright ripples in the wake of Ross's boat as we swept around the outlying islands, lying like green and golden clouds on the vast, sky-blue expanse of the sea. Ross handled the boat with quiet competence, not talking, steering close to dangerous reefs and buoys but never *too* close. The line between safety and risk for Ross seemed thinly but distinctly marked, and I appreciated it in the same way I had appreciated it when I had seen a good surgeon cut within a hairline of a vital organ, yet leave it intact, with as few blood vessels severed as possible. I had never known an outdoor man to seem so intelligent and competent; somehow, I associated work clothes and dark suntans with woodchoppers, cotton pickers, and other men who worked with their hands and not their minds. Steering his boat within a fraction of the danger area, making a swift run across the wake of a large boat that left us rocked for a fraction of a second—but I had expected to be half-capsized by such a swell—I saw an adventurous man, perhaps even a dangerous man. The quiet occupation of bird watcher seemed incredible for him.

He cut the motor suddenly, and in the shattering silence his voice sounded almost loud. "This is Sanctuary from the other side. Here, take my glasses"—he pointed to the sloping hillside—"and you can see my place, halfway up the hill there. Courtesy of the United States Forestry Division."

I picked out the little gray-painted cabin, and behind it, cresting the hills, the faint, faraway turret of the castle. I said, "You're closer than I thought."

"That's right. Sanctuary is really the mountaintop of what was probably once an undersea mountain," he said; "there's a flat beach on either side, but the center of the island is just one big, wooded hill. I've counted six hundred and nineteen different species that spend the summer here—not to mention migrants passing over."

I hadn't known that there were that many species of birds, and naïvely said so. He laughed.

"How did you decide to do this sort of work, Ross?" I asked.

Ross shrugged, and he suddenly seemed older than I had thought him. "How does anyone get into anything? I used to go out bird-watching as a kid. When I got out of the Army, I—" he hesitated—"wanted to get away from big cities. . . . I was a slum kid, and the mountains and hills looked good to me. I had visions of myself fighting forest fires and stalking the buffalo in the Wild West, I suppose. Instead, when they found out I knew birds, they sent me here, and . . ." Again, he shrugged. "Here I am."

"How long have you been here?"

He said, quietly, "Eleven years."

"I thought you were younger than that."

His smile was swift and flashing. "It's the quiet life keeps the wrinkles away."

"I don't know what to think. First you sound as if it were dull—and yet I don't suppose you'd stay if you didn't like it here," I said.

His blue-eyed gaze was disturbingly keen. "Do *you* like riding herd on a crazy teen-ager?"

"It's the work I'm trained to do," I said.

"And yet you could work in a big-city hospital—and I could be working in the Museum of Natural History," he retorted. "And here we are, anyhow—and how would you like some coffee? It's only a short walk up to my place." He saw me hesitate and said swiftly, "No etchings. Word of honor, Boy Scout Oath, and all that."

I laughed aloud. "I wasn't even thinking about that." The invitation had to be platonic; it was too forthright to be anything else.

He grinned and said, "Right. I have to live on the island with you—and would I make the mistake of alienating the first new face we've seen around here for three years?"

I asked, as he steadied the boat for me to step out, and then beached it, dragging it high across the sand, "Weren't there other nurses before me?"

"One fiftyish grandma with a voice like a file rasp," he said, "and I'm not surprised the kid couldn't stand her. And one high-heeled city girl, who collapsed shrieking the first time a seagull was indiscreet overhead."

I wondered about the girl who had died, but he did not mention her, and we walked slowly across the flat beach.

Beyond the path the beach widened slightly, and as I looked toward the wider place, something familiar in the rock-strewn pattern suddenly struck me, and I recognized the stretch of cliffs and sea caves where Deirdre had thrown her fit the other day.

He followed my glance.

"Let me warn you, incidentally," he said; "never come down here unless you're sure about the tides. Look." The strip of beach was rapidly narrowing with the incoming tide, and I began to realize why he had anchored his boat so high above the waterline. "The tide rushes like a millrace in the channel out there, and some of the sea caves are underwater at high tide. You can often find beautiful shells and odd little sea creatures—if you're interested in marine biology—at low tide. But if you get too interested and lose track of the tide, you might have to climb some damned steep cliffs, unless you want to drink salt water for supper. So if you want to explore the place, ask Brant or me about the tides."

58

"Not much chance of that," I said; "for some reason, Deirdre seems afraid of the place."

He nodded. "That's smart of her," he said. "Even though the kid can swim like a fish, it's not a place *I'd* care to be cut off in. If I were Brant, I'd want her to keep away. Come on, let's get that coffee. Watch your step on the path; it's a little steep here."

There was a spot halfway up to his cabin where the path widened and had been fenced off; he pointed outward and said, "I have a perfect view here. Nothing between me and Ireland."

"Peaceful," I said, conscious that the word was trite.

He nodded. "Now, yes. Before—well, I suppose you know our local horror story?"

"Jim told me there was a murder here about seven years ago. I gather one of the nearby islands is a gangsters' hideout or something."

"That's what they say. Personally, I think the poor devil fell overboard from some steamer—or jumped—got cut up in the propeller, and was washed ashore up here," Ross said, "but the local *gendarmerie* couldn't accept anything so undramatic." He looked at me, cautiously. "Or would you rather think of it as a murder too?"

"I hadn't thought of it one way or the other," I said, not altogether truthfully. Suddenly the time element caught my attention. "It happened about the same time Deirdre— lost her memory, didn't it?"

Did I imagine his sudden stillness? He said, "Did it? If so, it must have been an eventful summer."

I told myself I was imagining things. Certainly they would have explored *any* connection, even in time, between a murder and a crazed child. "And nothing much has happened since? But I gather there was another fatal accident only a few months ago?"

He said, with a trace of irritation, "Why do you think I warned you about those sea caves? The Fields woman must have been climbing around on them and fallen and smashed her head in."

"I thought she drowned," I said.

"Who told you that?"

59

"Why—I can't remember," I said, and wondered why it mattered.

But Ross was climbing again. "Come on," he said. "Let's go up while there's still light enough to admire the sunset from my window."

The cabin, which had two rooms—the one I saw evidently served as office, kitchen, and living room—was tidy in a masculine, shipshape sort of fashion that was so different from the way a woman would have created order. There were charts and thick books, and an open door led to a bedroom, in which I could see a shelf of books and a neatly made bed covered with Navy blankets.

He hooked up an electric percolator and spooned coffee into it, foraging in a refrigerator for a can of condensed milk and letting the coffee perk while I looked out the window, then turned to examine the books. We talked easily about birds and the various trees, the colors of the sunset, never again touching on anything personal. The coffee was good, and he hauled out a paper sack of fresh rolls, saying, "I picked these up from the grocery boat this morning; they should be good."

"They are," I said, sampling one. When we had finished our coffee, the room was darkening, and I rose. "I think I'd really better go," I said. "Deirdre will be needing me."

"I'll walk you back along the path," he said; "there's a shortcut, but it's sort of slippery unless you know your way very well." He hesitated, then said, "By the way—facilities are rather primitive; the john's a wooden shed in the rear. But if you'd care to inspect it, even out of curiosity . . ."

I laughed, saying, "I grew up on a backwoods farm myself." I ran my fingers over my hair; it was wildly windblown. He said, "Mirror?" and disappeared briefly into the bedroom and returned to hand me a small shaving mirror.

But while the door was open, I had seen, lying on the floor of the chaste room, a woman's nylon stocking. He followed my glance and suddenly lowered his eyes, but he said nothing; and what could I say? For heaven's sake, was I jealous; had I *wanted* to be invited into his bedroom? I concentrated on the mirror and on reducing my blond hair to order.

The path led over the crest of the hill and was steep in places, but navigable enough. Ross said, "I generally come this way. Now that you know me, drop in any time." He laughed. "The coffeepot's usually on."

I offered him my hand and said, "Thanks for a lovely afternoon."

He took it; then, suddenly, he leaned forward and, in amazement, I felt his lips brush my cheek. Before I could say anything, however, there was a crashing in the brush, and Jeremy, dragged by Thumbelina, burst out onto the path.

"Damn," said Ross in an undertone, as we broke apart.

I had to laugh, even while I was trying helplessly to evade Thumbelina's sloppy caresses, for Ross had drawn back and was edging away warily, circling. His face had turned suddenly savage, with a tight-drawn look I had never seen before.

"Call off that damned animal, you little devil!" he snarled at Jeremy.

Jeremy, tugging at Thumbelina's collar, finally hauled her off us, laughing his childish shrill laughter. "Down, Thumbie! Down, girl! Honest, Mr. Hunter, she won't hurt you."

I said, almost in apology—shocked by Ross's tone to the child—"The dog is really quite harmless."

He mopped his forehead, and I saw that he had literally gone white. He said, "Sorry I blew up; I have a sort of phobia of dogs. See you later, Susan." He went off down the path toward his cabin.

I walked along beside Jeremy and the now docile Thumbelina, while the little boy giggled. "That was a mean trick," said Jeremy. "I know Mister Hunter is scared of dogs, so I let Thumbie loose."

I said severely, trying to sound as I thought the prim-and-proper Hester would sound, "It was very rude of you."

"Aw, don't be a spoilsport," he begged, and against my will, I smiled, laying a hand on Thumbelina's shaggy coat.

"Just don't do it again—okay?" I said.

"All right," he promised; but his lip stuck out, and I wondered why he seemed to dislike Ross so much. Well, if Ross usually spoke to children like that, I couldn't blame

Jeremy much. I suddenly wondered whether Ross would have kissed me, without the interruption—and whether I had wanted him to.

Maybe I should be grateful to Thumbelina. It was certainly too soon to get involved with a man on Sanctuary Island—and, remembering that nylon stocking on the floor of his room, I wasn't sure I wanted to get involved with Ross anyhow.

I called to Thumbelina, "Here, girl! Come, Jeremy, I'll race you down to the shore!"

Chapter

Five

IT WAS the next afternoon, as Deirdre and I were coming in from swimming, that I had the first hint of what was to prove my major problem with Deirdre.

With robes over our swimsuits, we had come up through the front hall and were starting up the stairway when a door at the top of the landing opened and Martine McLeod started down the stairs.

I said politely, "Good afternoon, Mrs. McLeod," then broke off, for Deirdre had turned back, stumbling into me and half-knocking me over; she took me unawares and ran past me blindly, crashing into a small table and sending an ornament shattering. Appalled, I turned and flew after her, catching her at a corner of the hallway. I took her wrist, gently, but she flung me off with terrified strength and squirmed into the corner, her face against the wall, trying to make herself as small as possible.

Martine's voice was smooth and cold as ice as she said, "You clumsy, blundering fool! If this is the best you can do with her, Miss Moore," she was surveying the wreckage of broken china, "perhaps she'd better not be allowed to run about in here."

Her icy stare made me feel about two inches high. I longed for the authority of a uniform and cap instead of my old black swimsuit and frayed terrycloth robe. "I'm very sorry, Mrs. McLeod; Deirdre has never behaved like this before." I turned back to Deirdre, who was crouched in the corner, sobbing. "What's the matter, honey?" I pleaded. "Come on. Come with Susan."

Deirdre looked quickly over her shoulder, saw Martine, and buried her face in the corner again as if she were trying to press her whole slender body through the wall. Such storms of sobbing racked her that I felt she would fly asunder. Behind me I heard the bell and Martine's cold voice giving orders:

"Have this mess cleaned up at once. As you can see, Miss Deirdre's been on another of her violent fits. Miss Moore, if you can't control her better than that—"

I disliked discussing Deirdre in front of her, but I had to say, "Mrs. McLeod, that is hardly fair. Deirdre was not violent; something frightened her, and she ran, without looking where she was going. She is a child, remember." What was a broken ornament or two, contrasted with a child's obvious terror? I finally coaxed Deirdre, clinging to me, to turn around! Her head buried in my shoulder, she advanced, step by slow step, along the hallway.

"Take her to her room and lock her in," Martine commanded, and at the sound of her voice Deirdre suddenly shrieked again wildly and struggled.

It took all my strength to hold the frenzied girl, who had the strength of a woman for all her frailty. I appealed, "*Please,* Mrs. McLeod!"

"Are you trying to say—" but the rest was lost, for at the first sound of her mother's voice Deirdre began shriek and writhe in my arms again, and all my attention had to go to trying to control her. She broke away for a moment, ducked back, circled, making a wide circle around her mother. Martine backed away, her mouth opening in a sudden wide O of terror, but Deirdre, looking like a trapped animal, suddenly darted under Martine's outstretched arm and fled up the stairs. I sped after her, disregarding Martine's call, but on the first landing I sighed with relief for Deirdre was heading for her own rooms. I hurried on up the other flights of stars, reaching Deirdre's room almost as the girl slammed the door behind her. I went in. She was not in the playroom. She was not in the bedroom. In the bathroom, panic clutching at me, I finally found her crouched behind the shower curtain, still trembling.

"Deirdre, Deirdre," I soothed, "come out, dear. It's all right; don't cry. No one will hurt you. Tell me what frightened you."

She resisted my touch at first, then let me lead her out

64

of the bathroom. She swallowed hard, seeming to struggle for speech, and finally got out, "H-h-has she gone?"

"Who, darling?"

"Has she *gone?*"

Anything to quiet her. "Yes. There's no one here but me, Deirdre. It's Susan. It's all right, dear."

She clung to my hands until the bones ached. "She won't come up here? You promise? Promise?"

"I promise." Who, I wondered? Her *mother?* Had the mere sight of Martine roused Deirdre to such a frenzy of terror? I soothed her, promising again and again that no one except myself was there, and finally she lay on my shoulder like a sleepy child, her sobs subsiding to long, sighing breaths. Like a child, docile, she let me take off her robe and her bathing suit and run a warm bath for her. I put her into the bath, hoping the warm water would relax her, and I was rewarded by seeing the cold, tense, bluish look leave her limbs and face. For the first time she let me help her bathe and shampoo the salt water from her fine hair; I toweled her dry and dressed her in pajamas and brought her, with towel-wrapped hair, to sit by the bed; then I rang for Carla and asked her to bring up a cup of hot tea for the girl, and as an afterthought, I asked for some coffee for myself.

"Did she have another of her crazy fits, Miss?" Carla asked, looking at the girl curiously. Deirdre, hearing the words, started and began to sob again. Almost roughly, I shoved Carla out of the room.

"You mustn't talk like that in front of her," I ordered.

"She's balmy, Miss; she doesn't understand a word you say."

"She does understand," I aid severely, "and you are not to speak that way in front of her again. Miss Deirdre had a fright and got chilled. Please bring some hot tea at once."

Carla said sullenly, "Yes, Miss Moore," and left. I returned to Deirdre, who was lying on her bed sobbing, her head in the pillow. She sat up, shaking all over, as I came in; then, with a long sigh, she fell back.

"Oh, Susan. I was afraid it was—I was afraid—"

"Never mind," I said quickly; "it's me."

"She called me crazy!" Deirdre was weeping softly still, the tears streaming down her white face. "Susan, am I crazy? Does *everybody* think I'm crazy?"

I sat down on the bed beside her. I said soothingly, "I think you were very frightened, and you were not quite acting the way people expect you to act; so they didn't understand."

"I'm not crazy; I'm not!"

I did not answer directly. "Why were you so frightened, Deirdre?"

But she shut her mouth in the stubborn line I was beginning to know. "You won't believe me. You'll call me crazy and a liar and you'll hit me and pinch me and shake me and shake me and shake me and shake me. . . ."

I could not let this go on. "I certainly will do nothing of the kind," I assured her. "Hop into bed, now. All I'm going to do to you is put you into that bed and give you a cup of nice hot tea. It will warm you up. We don't want you to catch cold."

Carla brought the tea tray, with a pot of tea and one of coffee, to which someone had added a stack of thin bread and butter and a plate of cookies. I asked Deirdre matter-of-factly, "Do you like lemon in your tea, or milk and sugar?"

"Milk and sugar," she said, then suddenly looked at the tray with suspicion. "Did *she* send it up?"

This took me off guard. "Did *who*—"

"Mrs. Meadows sent it up, Miss," Carla said quickly.

Deirdre said, with a soft sight, "Oh, *that's* all right," and reached for a cookie. She sugared her own tea.

When Carla had gone, Deirdre looked sharply at me and said, "I thought *she* sent it. She'd like to poison me. She'd like to kill me, like she did—like she di-di-did—"

I said, quickly, "Eat your cookie, Deirdre. And drink up that tea while it's hot, now."

She obeyed, sighing. The color was beginning to come back into her cheeks. She drank two cups of tea and I persuaded her to eat some bread and butter and some of the cookies, and after a while she asked if I would play a game of parcheesi with her. I agreed, but while I was getting the board and pieces, Deirdre got out of bed, and I found her rummaging in the closet.

"What are you doing?"

She came back to bed meekly enough, but under her arm was a large baby doll. She tucked it carefully into bed beside her. Under the other arm was a huge, fluffy teddy bear; she set him carefully on the pillow. I watched her arrange them, startled.

She said, apologetically, "I know I'm too big for dolls. I just feel better when they're here." She stroked the doll's curly hair, and I watched her, puzzled. "Then if anyone tries to come in, in the night, and—and pinch me and shake me and—and—" she broke off, her voice strangling again, and I quickly reassured her, mentally reassessing the case.

Paranoid suspicions too? An abnormal fear of her mother, fear of poison, fear that some mysterious someone would come into her room and physically attack her? I persuaded her to sit up and play a game of parcheesi, which she won; but she kept breaking off to stroke the doll's hair or fondle the fur of the teddy bear; and when her supper was brought up, later, I had to reassure her, again, that Mrs. Meadows had fixed the tray for her, even offering, if she wished, to ring the bell for Mrs. Meadows and ask her.

"No. I believe *you*," she said, cuddling down between her dolls and reaching for her soup spoon.

I sat on in the room, even after she had fallen asleep, a little afraid that she would awaken and go into another spasm of paranoid fear. Was this one of those cyclic cases where the patient would be perfectly normal for weeks at a time, then, beginning with mild fears, go into greater and greater spasms of violence, and finally turn raving mad and have to be restrained, gradually quieting again to normalcy?

If so, I knew I must have a doctor on call; if nothing else, I would need authority to administer sedatives or tranquilizers when necessary. Tomorrow I would demand an interview with Martine herself, and insist upon it. For Heaven's sake, I did not even know the name of the family physician, in the event Deirdre should have some perfectly ordinary illness like a cold or the measles!

When Deirdre finally slept, and I was certain by her slow, regular breathing that she would not awaken for a time at least, I decided to go to my own room, change into pajamas and a robe, and return, to sleep that night on the couch in Deirdre's playroom. If I had had a sedative to give her, it might have been different, but without medical supervision I could not give even the mildest of sleeping pills.

I came out into the hall, and started as a white form, moving ghostlike through the shadows, glided without sound toward me. I stifled a cry; then common sense came to the rescue.

"Mrs. McLeod, you startled me."

"I've been waiting here for a long time," Martine said. The light on her face was pale, making her ravaged beauty striking with its sharp definition of light and shade. I remembered reading that one of her most famous roles had been the sleepwalking scene in the Verdi opera based on Shakespeare's *Macbeth*.

I suddenly felt pity for this woman; standing here in the dark and dismal hallway, perhaps for hours, waiting for news of the daughter who feared her so, refusing perhaps even to knock at the door, lest she frighten or disturb the sick girl further. I felt more friendly toward Martine, and said gently, "I suppose I really should have sent you word before this, Mrs. McLeod; Deirdre is quiet, now, and fast asleep. But I won't leave her alone; I'll change into my night things and sleep on the couch in her playroom, so that if she wakes up and is frightened in the night, she won't be alone."

Martine said hoarsely, "What did that little demon say about me?" She took a step toward me, and I actually fell back, so threatening was her white face. "Whatever she said, she lied!"

I was puzzled, anxious to reassure her. "Believe me, she said nothing of any importance. She seems abnormally afraid of you, at the moment, Mrs. McLeod, but you mustn't be troubled by that. Disturbed or emotionaly ill people often turn against the very ones who are dearest

68

to them when they are well. You mustn't be upset. I know how a mother must feel when her child seems to reject her, but remember that Deirdre is sick—"

"Whatever she might have said, it's one of her crazy lies," Martine repeated, and her face, fierce and haggard in its beauty, reminded me of some predatory eagle. "She's crazy, and if you believe her you'll only be getting yourself in trouble!"

She turned and swept away from me, and I felt my newfound pity for the woman evaporating. Afraid for Deirdre? Not she! She was only afraid of what the girl might have said about her! Was the woman *completely* selfish, then?

At least, though, it explained why Martine did not visit Deirdre in her rooms or ask to have the girl brought to her. If Deirdre threw this sort of tantrum every time Martine came near her, I could understand Martine's being unwilling to risk such a scene.

But when I was in my own room, brushing my teeth and changing into my night things, a sudden and disturbing thought hit me.

Deirdre, so they said, had been mad for seven years; during the first three of those years, she had not spoken, and when she had begun to speak again, she had lost her memory. If the girl were so obviously mad, then why on earth was Martine still worried about what irrational accusations Deirdre might make? What did it matter whether Deirdre accused her mother of trying to poison her or accused the Queen of England of spying on her from a postage stamp?

And Deirdre's accusations had been curiously self-consistent. . . .

Was it possible that Deirdre had some valid reason to fear her mother?

I was still far from the conclusion that was to steal over me, with increasing conviction, in the days to come. It simply occurred to me that Martine, faced with an uncontrollable child given to violent temper tantrums and spasmodic, convulsive fits, might have treated Deirdre harshly —she might have struck or shaken the child, who was already irrationally frightened, and given her cause for fear.

I told myself sharply that I was becoming almost paranoid myself. Because I disliked Martine, because I considered her a spoiled, selfish woman, I was taking seriously the accusations of a child obviously disturbed and violent.

And yet—*The lady doth protest too much, methinks?*

Susan, I told myself angrily, *you're beginning to be affected by the whole atmosphere of this big nuthouse. Forget it and get back to your patient. Tomorrow she may wake up afraid of you. . . . Then how will you feel?*

Chapter
Six

My MISGIVINGS proved vain. When Deirdre woke in the morning, she seemed her usual cheery self and made no reference, even obliquely, to her fright of yesterday. I wondered if she had forgotten it. A psychotherapist might have asked her; he might have probed the episode. I wasn't a psychotherapist, and didn't intend to get into trouble by trying to be one. I accepted her docility, and, while never relaxing my watchfulness, I was again surprised at the sensible, tractable way in which Deirdre behaved most of the time.

I had decided it was useless to ask Martine about Deirdre again, but when I attempted to see Brant McLeod, I was told that he had gone on a business trip to the mainland. So, especially since Deirdre seemed to be in a spell of calm, I put off again the problem of consulting a doctor. I took advantage of one quiet afternoon, however, to seek Mrs. Meadows in her own rooms and ask her who was the doctor in charge of Deirdre's case.

"I really wouldn't know, Miss; although, come to think of it, about two years ago she had a touch of the flu and a doctor came from the mainland—the same doctor that looks after the little boy. Now what was his name?" She wrinkled her downy old brow. "I can't remember. You might ask the little chap's Nanny; she'd know, of course."

Once again I was struck with the enormity of this great castle. Deirdre and I could literally come and go for days at a time without seeing anyone except servants. And yet there was a married couple, such as they were—old Mr. McLeod and Martine—there was Brant, and whatever affairs he had; there was a little boy who evidently lived alone with his nurse, for somehow I couldn't imagine that

Martine was a very attentive mother, even to her normal child. Yet we might have been in separate villages, isolated from one another. It simply was not natural. No wonder Deirdre had grown up a little mad, with not even a substitute for normal family life!

We went out early for a swim that day and found that Jeremy and Thumbelina were playing on the beach, while Hester Cairncross, seated on an enormous beach towel, was watching them with an indulgent smile on her plain, broad face. She looked up, somewhat apprehensively, as I approached, but before either of us could say a word, Jeremy gave a shriek of delight.

"Deedee!"

He ran toward us at full speed. I watched Deirdre apprehensively; if she had turned against her family, might she not attempt to attack, or flee from, her small half-brother? But instead, her delighted pixie smile transformed her face to radiance.

"Jerry!"

They hugged each other rapturously, both talking at once. Deirdre looked apprehensively at me then, but Jeremy dragged his sister bodily toward the edge of the sand.

"Deedee, come see my castle. Come see how I can swim now? You're not sick any more, are you?" He would not let go her hand, and I was afraid to demand that they release one another. I followed closely as they knelt side by side on the warm sand.

Deirdre looked up at me, pleadingly. "Please, Susan, please. Don't make Jerry go away from me. Not you too."

Apprehensive still, I gave reluctant consent. "You may play on the beach here, but before you go in swimming, ask me so that I can go in with you."

I moved out of earshot of the children, watching carefully, but Deirdre appeared entirely absorbed in the small boy, and I realized that I had never known her to go into a tantrum fit without some immediate triggering cause; if she had been going to have a fit at the sight of Jeremy, she'd have already had it. I sat down beside Hester, frowning slightly.

Hester, too, looked somewhat apprehensive. "Eh, nurse,

72

I don't like it. Both Mr. Brant and old Mr. Alexander have ordered that the children aren't to be together."

"They're not alone together," I said, "and I'm watching her carefully; don't worry."

"Miss Moore . . ."

"Susan—please. It's silly, when we live under the same roof, Hester."

She smiled. "Susan, then. What ails the poor child? I'd a notion at first when I came here that she was deaf and dumb, but deaf and dumb she's not, and no one will tell me a word of it."

I said, "I'm not certain. She is mentally disturbed, of course, but I'm not sure why; and I'm certain she's not violent. But I wanted to talk to you, Hester, and ask you; who is the children's doctor? I can't ask Mrs. McLeod, for she refuses to discuss the girl at all with me. And Mr. Brant McLeod is on the mainland."

Hester considered. "Well, there's a Doctor Robertson, a decent old body, comes from the mainland when the wee boy is ill," she said, "so that if Miss Deedee were to get a cold or some such thing, he'd no doubt look at her chest and the like. Though I don't know as he'd be much good for what else ails her," she added dubiously. "Wouldn't you think, indeed, they'd have one of these fine psychiatrist persons to look after her?"

I didn't think I was being indiscreet by agreeing most heartily with her about that.

"Still, I'd daresay they have their reasons, Miss."

I asked, "How long have you been with Jeremy?"

"Four years."

"And has Deirdre been as she is now, all that time?"

"No, indeed. When I first came to this place, she couldn't talk plain at all, and I heard she was deaf and dumb, like. Changed, she has, most marvelous, since then, and I do believe poor Miss Margo, she that was drowned, did the most of it with her." Hester sighed, adding, "But after that, I heard she'd got worse again; I used to take the little laddie to see his sister every night and have supper, but since Miss Margo died, Mrs. McLeod gave strict orders that the children were to be kept apart." She looked with disquiet on her charge, but the two were hap-

73

pily adding turret upon turret to an elaborate sand castle. "Unnatural, I call it, for a brother and sister not to be allowed to play together, and where's the harm? And that Mrs. McLeod—it's not my place to say so, Miss Susan, but it's in my mind she neither knows nor cares what's going on with the girl, and old Mr. McLeod—well, if you want my opinion, which you probably don't, I think he's as daft as the girl!"

"He seemed sharp enough, the one night I met him," I protested.

"Well, what old man who wasn't daft would marry a woman young enough to be his granddaughter?" she demanded. "For he must be rising eighty, and Mrs. McLeod isn't half of that. If she'd married Mr. Brant, now, it would be different. It's in my mind, she married the old gentleman for his money thinking she'd be free of him in a year or two. But there, I shouldn't speak ill of her," she added quickly, and I had to smile at her self-conscious efforts not to gossip. "Except that I don't believe she would know or care if the wee lad saw his sister now and again, and as they say, what the eye doesn't see, the heart doesn't grieve for. Or are you thinking that would be dishonest, now?"

I shook my head. "I think it would do Deirdre no end of good to have some natural companionship and someone young to play with," I said sincerely; "and she and her brother seem happy together."

"Then let's have them together, Susan," Hester said earnestly, "because the way the wee boy grieves for his sister would make the angels weep. Look," she pointed, "there they are, playing with that great brute of a dog. Don't they look happy now?"

The children romped together on the beach with the dog; when, later, they wanted to swim, both Hester and I went in with them, each watching her charge carefully—somewhat hampered by the splashy flounderings of Thumbelina, who wanted to swim almost on top of Jeremy. When it finally began to grow chilly on the beach, and Jeremy, with nurse and dog, had been taken off for his supper, Deirdre slipped a shy arm around my waist. It was the first time she had touched me of her own accord.

"Thank you, Susan. I've had so much fun; I can't remember when I've been so happy. Not since Jeremy and Thumbie and I used to play together all the time."

For the next several days, all was peaceful and quiet; Brant returned from the mainland, but I scarcely saw him. Ross Hunter telephone one afternoon and invited me to a movie on the mainland; I accepted, and I enjoyed his company, but there was no more to it than that. When he said good night, he took it for granted that we would meet again on my next afternoon off, and I saw no reason why not.

This time we went walking in the woods on Sanctuary Island, and he showed me some of the haunts of the strange, wild birds that made their nests here. We got back late, dirty and disheveled after hours spent scrambling through underbrush and climbing dead trees to peer into nearby nests. After we had had coffee in his little cabin, he walked me back across the steep, shortcut path toward Duncarlie Castle. I had a curious sense of *déjà vu* as he stopped short, suddenly, and put his arms out toward me; but this time there was no interruption, and, almost in one dreamlike motion, I felt his lips on mine.

When he let me go I felt vaguely dizzied, and my head was spinning. No doubt it was just that I was new—and available. But I had been kissed before this, and it had never disturbed me so. It took me unawares.

He said, very softly, "Next time—perhaps we needn't go bird scrambling to get to this point?"

"Not so fast," I said, shaken. I wanted to think it over a bit. Was I simply falling, on the rebound, into the arms of the first accessible male?

He shrugged slightly. "I can wait," he said, and gave my hand a lighthearted squeeze. "Until next week, then, Susan."

He turned back toward his cabin, and I continued down the path with a curious sense that my feet were not quite touching the ground. I told myself firmly not to lose my head— *Do you want to be another stray nylon stocking on his bedroom floor?*

"Talking to yourself, Miss Moore? Penny for your thoughts," a deep voice said, and Brant McLeod stepped

75

out on the path beside me. "Forgive me for intruding," he said, "but I thought I'd wait until Hunter was out of the way. May I offer my escort back to the gates?" His tone was almost sarcastic. "Where I was brought up, a gentleman usually sees a lady to her door, but perhaps Ross isn't aware of these niceties."

"Or perhaps he knows he wouldn't be welcome on your property," I retorted sharply, and Brant's mouth twisted.

"Hell, I've got nothing against Ross, except that he's a damned pest," he said. "What the devil does he want to be hanging around here for anyhow? Bird-watching—what sort of an occupation is that for a man?"

"The government evidently considers it worth paying his salary for," I retorted.

Brant said thoughtfully, "Spitfire mood today, eh?"

I thought, without saying, *Maybe bird-watching is no job for a man, but what are YOU doing—except waiting around for the old gentleman to die so you can inherit his money? And maybe even his young wife?*

As if he had followed my thoughts, Brant said, disturbingly, "Not that I have much right to talk. Duncarlie runs itself without me, between Lowden and Mrs. Meadows. How do you find Deirdre these days, Susan?"

I hardly noticed that he had used my first name. "She seems much calmer and happier," I replied.

"I thought some young company would do her good," Brant said. We walked along in companionable silence for a while; then, as we came to the top of the path leading down to the rocky stretch of beach with the sea caves, he asked suddenly, "Have you been down here yet?"

"Not yet."

"The tide's dead low, and it's safe enough. Would you like to see the place? There's a little stiff rock scrambling to do, but I don't imagine you'd mind that."

"No. I'm fairly sure on my feet."

Holding on with my hands where he told me, I got down the sharp slope behind him, and we came out on a forty-foot-wide strip of sandy beach, strewn with sharp boulders and rocks. The cliff overshadowed it, looming darkly and cutting the evening sunlight away. In the cliff there were gaping black patches like open, hungry mouths.

76

"Like to go in? It's safe enough, at low tide," Brant said, and produced a flashlight from his pocket. I hesitated, then followed him, treading carefully on the sharp, rocky path. Inside, the sea cave felt cold and dank, and the floor was sandy and wet underfoot.

He flashed his light on the walls, showing me the strange sea creatures, like limpets, that clung to the rock ledges. "At high tide this is all underwater," he said. "I was almost trapped here once, as a child, and I only managed to get out by climbing the cliff face up to the higher cave and waiting for the water to go down. It's not a hard climb"—he showed me the steep slope and the dark opening through which the palest lasting light filtered—"but if you lost your nerve or your grip, you'd get a nasty fall; and nobody could swim in the riptide on this side of the island."

Suddenly there was a deep, hollow, booming sound that echoed and reechoed. Brant and I swung around and looked at each other, startled, in the gathering darkness.

"What on earth was that?" I demanded. "It sounded like nothing on earth!"

"I'm not sure. Hush; there it is again. . . ." We heard the sound go rolling around the long hollow cave again, echoing from wall to wall in grotesque and distorted sound-waves. Suddenly Brant laughed aloud as Thumbelina, barking loudly, rushed from the back of the cave. The open hollow space had distorted the dog's deep baying into something unearthly.

"There's your spook—or should I say Hound of the Baskervilles," he laughed. Then he grew sober. "I hope Jerry hasn't started exploring down here; he's too young to take note of the tides!"

"I have seen Thumbelina wandering around the island alone," I assured him.

He bent, petting the dog. "I have, too."

We came out on the strip of beach, and Brant glanced at his watch. "We'd better go back; the tide's on the turn, and"—he indicated his good trousers—"I'm not wearing my cliff-climbing kit this time."

I asked, as we walked toward the end of the beach nearer to the castle and to our own strip of beach, "Why is Deirdre afraid of this place?"

He hesitated, then said, "I'm not sure. But it was here we found her—that day, after she'd been lost.'

"Could she have been trapped in the upper caves and had a fright from that, do you suppose?"

"We've never known."

"And this was where the man was found murdered—about that same time? Could Deirdre have seen the dead man—even the murder, perhaps?" I asked impetuously. Brant's face turned suddenly hard and cold.

"You *do* have a romantic imagination, don't you, Miss Moore?"

"Well, I understand that Margo Fields also died here," I retorted quickly; "the place seems to have a dangerous reputation."

He stopped dead in his tracks. It was getting dark and I could just see the stubborn set of his jaw. "Are *you* afraid to be here?" he asked suddenly.

A premonitory shudder suddenly ran over me, and I thought of the old saying "A goose walked over my grave." Then the moment vanished, and I saw that Brant was laughing behind the stern mask.

"No," I said; "I'm not afraid." And then, prompted by God knows what imp of sarcasm, I added, "How could I possibly be afraid—with *you* to protect me?"

He took a step toward me, and a sudden, not unpleasant sting of fright mingled with amazement went through me as he suddenly seized my elbows, bent, and kissed me, roughly, on the lips.

"There," he said, drawing away. "Was that what you wanted?"

I stepped back, outraged to the very bone. How *dared* he? Or was it one of his outrageous jokes? I felt shaken, dazed, and still somewhat incredulous. The next moment, with infinite remote politeness and an ironic gravity, he offered me his arm.

"Come along, Miss Moore. As I say, a gentleman always escorts a lady to her door after he has kissed her—and I thought you might appreciate the contrast in these things."

I pulled my arm free of him and stood facing him, almost too indignant to speak. I knew my eyes were snapping fire. The words were on my lips to reduce him to withered fragments. . . . Then suddenly I knew he was waiting for them; he had been baiting me. I turned my back, with what dignity I could muster, and stalked toward the path. At the top of the path I looked back, but Brant was standing where I had left him, unmoving.

Damn him, I thought viciously; *I hope he has to swim home.*

Chapter
Seven

ONE OF the few rooms in Duncarlie Castle not equipped
with a house telephone was Deirdre's. I had been three
weeks on Sanctuary Island when Carla summoned me,
one morning, away from the breakfast table to the phone
in the hall.

"Telephone, Miss Moore."

I smiled at Deirdre over the toast. "Back in a minute."

"Ross Hunter here," came the familiar voice. "How
would you like to see one of our rarest birds this afternoon,
Susan?"

"Birds . . . ?"

"You know. The things that fly. My reason for being on
this island; remember?" He chuckled. "Yesterday I spotted
an American golden plover—*Pluvialis dominica dominica,*
if you want to be technical, which I don't suppose you do.
They breed on the Canadian Barren Grounds, then mi-
grate east to Labrador, and southward over the Atlantic,
winding up somewhere in Argentina. I've spotted this par-
ticular group every year for the last three years, and they
always stay here for about forty-eight hours before moving
on southward. I want to check and see if there are any of
my banded birds in the group—statistics like that are what
the Forestry Service pays me for, you know."

I said, on impulse, "Couldn't I bring Deirdre too? She's
so interested in birds—"

I could feel the rejection in his voice as he said, "Don't
they ever let you away from that kid?"

"Of course they do. But honestly, Ross, you should see
the charts she keeps on migratory birds. She was talking
about this very kind of plover just the other day," I remembered, "and she'll be so interested."

"Well . . ." He hesitated again.

I said, rather stiffly, "Of course, if you'd rather not . . ."

"As a matter of fact," he said, and the warm chuckle was back in his voice, "I'd rather not. The birds were just a good excuse . . . and if you can't guess the reason, you're not as smart as you look. But listen here; why don't you take the kid to see the birds this morning, if she's really interested—and if you can trust her not to try to grab them, or scare them away, or shy stones at them."

Indignantly, I said, "If you'd watched her on her bird expeditions, you wouldn't say that. She's as likely to harm a bird as—as you are!"

"Well, you should know," he said, not interested. He told me exactly how to reach the part of the island where the group of birds was resting, and finished, "Then I'll see you some time this afternoon—*without* the kid. All right?"

"I can arrange that," I promised, and hung up, my heart light, only vaguely troubled by Ross's attitude to my charge. Heaven knows, when the child's own mother wouldn't come near her, what opinion *could* anyone have who didn't know the girl?

Deirdre was as excited as I'd predicted when I told her of Ross's call, and she glance with a professional's eye at the overcast sky. "Good weather for them to rest in; they can find more insects and things than when the sun is shining." She danced about, lightheartedly collecting her field glasses, her Audubon guide, and the notebook she kept as a record of her sightings. "I got just a glimpse of one last year," she said; "I thought some of them must visit Sanctuary, but I was never quite sure."

The place Ross had described as the resting-place of the birds was a sizable distance into the interior of the island; but I had already learned that Deirdre's fears extended only to the stretch of land on the seaward side, with the rock cliffs and the sea caves. We walked along the shore at first, and Deirdre raised her binoculars to her eyes and trained them on a hovering bird which suddenly plummeted to the surface of the water and rose again.

"There's a gannet."

"I thought they were all gulls."

81

"We have gulls, too," she said. "Look, there's a herring gull. You can tell the difference because a herring gull takes a fish in his bill, while an osprey takes it in his talons, and a gannet dives down from a height. A cormorant swims like a duck and does a funny little somersault into the water to catch a fish. And the skua gull—I've only seen them once or twice—doesn't fish at all, but chases the other gulls and scares them into disgorging their fish so he can snap it up."

I listened with respect and fascination as this girl, whose mother persisted in treating her as an ineducable lunatic, talked on knowledgeably about sea and land birds.

"There's a great crested grebe." She noted it carefully in her notebook after showing me the bird through her glasses. "They're seen oftener in the British Isles, I've read. But I've seen them here at least a dozen times."

As we located the muddy slope, near a wooded pool, where Ross had seen the birds, I said, "You could learn a lot from Ross Hunter."

Her face darkened with the now-familiar sullen look, but all she said was, "He doesn't like me." She raised her binoculars again. Around us the forest was quiet, with only the soft, all-pervasive background of chirps and twitters. I listened for a moment, enchanted, to a soft whit-whit-whit-whit-wheeeeeeety, and wondered, aloud, how many birds lived on Sanctuary Island.

"I have four hundred and seventeen pairs spotted for last year in my notebook," Deirdre said, "which means that's the number of singing males I noticed. Of course I may have counted one more than once. But it's supposed to be one of the more heavily populated bird sanctuaries. It's in all the encyclopedias, you know."

I hadn't known. I asked suddenly, "When did you start to get interested in bird-watching, Deirdre?"

I knew at once it had been the wrong question, for her face furrowed in that strange, questioning effort. "I can— I ca-ca-can't remember," she said. "I used to—I used to—"

"Never mind, dear," I said quickly.

But she struggled on and finally, triumphantly, said, "I used to go out with my daddy! When I was little! *He* liked birds!"

With an effort, I concealed my amazement. They had told me that Deirdre displayed no memory whatever of any event before the episode when she had been lost, for a night and a day, somewhere on the island. Was the amnesia beginning to lighten? I felt like asking, cautiously, what else she remembered. A psychologist would have probed, but I feared setting off another explosion of tears or fright. Good God, I wasn't qualified to handle this girl without some help from a psychiatrist! So I only said, without emphasis, "That must have been nice," and turned away again. "Do you see that famous golden plover anywhere?"

We had kept our voices lower than the birdsong; she drew a soft breath of excitement, pointing to the edge of the pool; then, quickly and generously, she handed me the binoculars. The powerful glasses seemed to bring the flowers and leaves at the edge of the pool so close that I felt I could have touched one of the delicately veined ferns. And there, in the mud at the very edge of the pool, was something else—the clear print of a high-heeled shoe that had sunk deep in the mud.

Here? Martine certainly would never stand around in the mud. I wore sandals for my expeditions with Deirdre, and these prints had never been made by Hester's canvas sneakers or Mrs. Meadows' sturdy ground-grippers. One of the maids, on an off moment, picking flowers? Most of them seemed more disposed to spend their spare time on the mainland, going over with Old Jim on his biweekly trips, or catching the small mailboat shuttle that carried passengers daily. But it was a minor mystery; what sort of woman would wear spike heels out here in the woods?

We waited patiently for more than an hour, Deirdre and I passing back and forth the binoculars, listening to the distant birdsong, Deirdre now and then making a brief note in her books. Deirdre was ecstatic when she finally pointed out the plover to me. I found it a small, unremarkable bird not too unlike a partridge and hardly as golden as the name would suggest.

All morning, there had been stray gleams of fragmentary sun from the shifting overcast; but the sun finally went in, and by the time Deirdre and I returned for lunch, a dull, thick, gray overhead hung drearily over Sanctuary Island, and wisps of fog were rolling inland from the sea. As I left Deirdre, cozily drawn up in the corner of her playroom with Mrs. Meadows setting out one of their checker games, I almost regretted my decision to go.

"I'm tempted to stay on and teach you two to play gin rummy," I said, and Mrs. Meadows flashed me a quick wink. "I'll teach the little minx to play poker instead," she said cheerfully. "We'll use the counters from her parcheesi game—and don't you stand there looking so surprised, Miss; my old father taught me to play the best game of two-handed draw poker in three states, when I was a girl Miss Deirdre's age."

I left them over the cards, shivering a little as I drew my raincoat around my shoulders. Brrrr, what a miserable day! Passing through the heavily carpeted lower hallway, I heard through the open library door the raised, rather querulous voice of old Alexander McLeod.

"But where *is* Martine? Why on earth would she go out on a day like this? For Heaven's sake, Lowden, my wife must be somewhere—in her rooms, perhaps, or in the west wing!"

Then I heard Lowden's soft voice repeating, "Mrs. McLeod is not in her rooms, sir, and she hasn't been to the kitchens. Shall I try to reach her on all the house phones, Mr. Alexander?"

I pushed open the heavy door for myself and escaped down the steps. The air was cold and damp, and I walked quickly along the muddy path, back across the steep short-cut that led over the knife ridge that rose, like a spine, in the middle of the island, toward Ross's cabin. The mud was slippery, and I had to watch my step as I climbed. So intent was I on my path that, as I surmounted the ridge, pausing to breathe before the descent, I almost blundered into someone coming up the path from the other direction.

"Clumsy—!" said a sharp voice.

I drew back, gasping, "Excuse me!" Then, as I raised my eyes, I blinked in disbelief. Martine McLeod stood before me, coatless and hatless, her skirt and sweater damp and crumpled, her hair dripping with the fog, and her stockings torn and muddy.

84

She looked so unlike herself that I could not help immediately asking, "Is there something wrong, Mrs. McLeod? What on earth—"

"Nothing at all," she said with asperity; "I suppose I can go for a walk as well as anyone else, Miss Moore?"

I hastened to apologize. "I'm sorry. It's only . . . Your shoes are so muddy—I thought you might have fallen. . . ." Trying to make a joke out of it, I went on, "Trust a nurse to smell trouble, Mrs. McLeod. If I let your daughter go out for a walk without a coat and hat, and catch her death of cold, I'd never hear the last of it!"

She said, somewhat mollified but still looking at me with sharp annoyance, "I obviously didn't expect the rain, Miss Moore. And what are you doing out in it, if I may ask?"

I was suddenly reluctant to speak of Ross to her. "Just out for a walk, too," I said.

She surveyed me with her sharp eyes. "Hunter, I suppose. Just a friendly word of warning, Miss Moore: I suppose it's a lonely life here for a young woman—or a young man. But you'd probably be unwise to get mixed up with him seriously."

I assured her, feeling somewhat ironic, that I wasn't seriously involved with any man and didn't expect to be, wondering what business it was of hers anyway. And as she went off down the path toward the castle, I found myself looking after her with a jaundiced eye. Out for a walk and caught in the rain? Martine, the chic and *soignée?* Like fun!

Had *she* been down at Ross's cabin? And what on earth would she be doing there?

Susan Moore, I told myself firmly, *you are developing a very dirty mind.* I wrapped myself more snugly in my raincoat and went down the path, feeling sorry for Martine, who was stumbling home in her wet skirt and tottery, muddy high-heeled shoes.

In the little cabin, Ross had lighted an open fire that glowed with a pleasant heat as I pulled off my dripping raincoat. He himself was shirt-sleeved and barefoot, and he gestured to my muddy shoes. "Leave 'em at the door— Japanese style," he said. "It saves the broom workouts."

I shed my shoes and padded across the room in stockinged feet to curl up on the sofa at the opposite end. I was beginning to feel very comfortable with this relaxed, big, blond man, who was so like and yet so utterly unlike Raymond Grantham. *Chemistry,* I thought comfortably, *just chemistry; I happen to like big, blond men.*

He poured strong coffee generously laced with a dollop of Irish whisky. "That'll take the damp out of your bones," he said. "And you're not on duty, so no scruples about drinking. Be warned," he grinned, "I expect to get you comfortably tight, and I intend to extract your life story from you, Susan."

I sipped appreciatively. "There's not that much to extract. Pure vanilla, in fact. I grew up on a chicken farm, went to a small-town school, went away to nursing school, took up psychiatric nursing and worked two years in a mental hospital, decided I needed extra specialization as a surgical nurse too, and went in for a year at a Philadelphia hospital."

"And you wound up here," he mused. "How strange. I'd think you'd crave the big cities and bright lights; most small-town girls do."

"All a nurse sees of big cities are accident wards, ambulances, and emergency calls," I retorted, then was silent, thinking of the gray, damp day like this in Philadelphia when Raymond Grantham had gone out of my life forever.

Ross was watching, and he said softly, "Not all vanilla, eh, Susan?"

I shook my head, resolutely banishing the ghosts. "Bland diet. But what about you, Ross? *Your* life story would probably make better telling than mine."

He shrugged. "A little more highly seasoned, maybe. I told you I was a slum kid—grew up on the flats of Oakland, California. My parents called themselves Bohemians —nowadays it would be beatniks, I suppose. Just plain bums would be closer to it. My father fooled around with Zen Buddhism and wore a beard, and my mother wore sandals and adored health foods and took painting classes at the free colleges and never bothered with anything mundane like cooking or sweeping or dishwashing. I got to running around with a tough gang of kids around the water-front, and one day we broke in and stole a jalopy from a used-car lot and took off for Tijuana, just for the hell of it. End of Ross Hunter, second generation beatnik; enter Ross Hunter and the California Juvenile Courts. They sent me to a Forestry Camp instead of a reform school, and I fell in love with it. When they turned me loose at eighteen, I should have stuck with it. Instead I decided I'd try the big cities again, and hit Las Vegas. I worked in one of the tourist hotels for a while, until they found out I had a record; then I couldn't get a decent job, so I wound up working as a dealer in one of the gambling casinos. I didn't know it was run by the Syndicate until one night a fellow came in, had a run of luck at my table, and walked off with twenty thousand of the house's money. Somehow or other, word got around that the Syndicate guys caught up with him and took it back—the hard way. They found him lying in an alley with his throat cut. Then the word went out that the dealer was in for the same treatment—and I grabbed the first plane out of there. It happened to be going to Washington, D.C., and I wound up asking the Forestry Service for a job. They sent me out here—and here I am. I told you it was a lousy background. Ex-reform-school kid, probably people would think of me as ex-gambler—and hiding out from the Syndicate. A nice girl like you would probably be disgusted," he finished bitterly.

But it sounded to me more the story of a kid who had had hard luck than anthing blameworthy, and I told him so.

We had moved together, spontaneously, in the telling, and suddenly I found his lips firmly on mine, his arms around me. He said, blurrily, "I knew you'd understand. I was going to play it straight—let you think I was the average small-town good boy—but I wanted you to know the real score."

"Anyone who could blame you for the past . . . and after how many years here with a perfect record?" I said indignantly.

"Believe me, there are still people who would hold it against me," Ross said with a twist of his lip, "and I doubt if I'd be safe in Vegas even now. Those guys have long memories. No; I've found this a damn good place to lie low in."

I thought, incredulously; for a twenty-thousand-dollar loss at gambling, which they'd recovered in any case, would they still be after the dealer? It was possible; I knew nothing about such things; I didn't even like gangster movies or novels. It seemed incredible to be sitting across from a man who had lived through what sounded like the script for a gangster movie . . . but what an anticlimax for an ending! No gangster movie would be content to have the victim settle down peacefully for years and years, keeping a bird sanctuary. I let Ross kiss me again.

"You're about as probable a gangster as—as old man McLeod," I said, and forgot about gangsters and old stories for some time. When I finally drew apart from him, I was breathless and mussed, and my face was flushed.

He clung a minute, then quickly loosed me. "Sorry, Susan," he said softly; "I know. We won't rush things. I think I could use another cup of that Irish coffee. You?"

I nodded. "But without the whisky this time. Your system is entirely too effective, young man."

"It's meant to be," he said, disregarding me and pouring another splash of whisky into my coffee.

"I won't drink it. No, Ross; I mean it," I said, going to the small sink for a clean cup and pouring some coffee without whisky. I paused there, stopped cold. For on the kitchen floor, by the sink, was the muddy print of a woman's high-heeled shoe.

I suppose, in the long run, it's a good thing I saw it. I might have made an awful fool of myself, that very afternoon. But the sight stopped me cold, and I remembered Martine's words and her muddy shoes.

Jealousy? Or did she simply know him too well?

One could hardly blame Ross for trying. After all, Martine was a woman in her thirties, accustomed to fame and applause, yet buried here with an elderly, wheelchair-bound husband. Traditionally, such women were fair game for the amateur Casanova. As a nurse, I'd seen enough of human nature not to be shocked at common or garden-variety philandering. But somehow it destroyed the mood

88

of the afternoon. The coffee was bitter on my tongue, and somehow the sofa drawn up to the fire, the Irish whisky, the exchange of life histories, seemed almost too calculating to make an appeal to the senses.

And did I want to step into Martine's very muddy footprints?

Ross knew somehow, when I sat down with my coffee, that the magical mood of sympathy had been destroyed. We went on talking, but he did not kiss me again, and he did not object when, looking out into the heavy rain, I suggested that I had better start back.

"If it wasn't so windy, I'd run you around the island in my boat," he said, "but there are small-craft warnings up all over the coast. Looks like blowing a three-day gale. And it's high tide now; the riptide around the end of the island would probably capsize us. If you'll wait for low water, we'll try and make a run for it," he suggested, but I refused to wait. I wanted the walk back, cold rain and all, to clear my head of his whisky, his story—and his kisses.

It was, indeed, a three-day gale. The next morning the wind was savage, lashing around the turrets of Duncarlie Castle with a wild, shrill moaning noise that made me feel, snug in my bed, as if I had stepped into a movie set equipped with sound, all set up for *Wuthering Heights*. Deirdre was listless and disconsolate, staring idly out the window; there was no possibility of walking or swimming. She turned over all her bird books, idly, tried to settle down to reading, refused to play any game, and finally went to her closet and pulled out the doll I had seen before and a large tin biscuit box. She looked at me hesitantly before she opened it.

"You're going to think I'm awfully babyish."

I filed that away mentally. Maybe playing dolls at Deirdre's age was babyish. But I had known retarded children in plenty—and they didn't *know* it was babyish; they just did it. I said calmly, "I played with dolls myself until I was fourteen or so."

"Well, I really like making dresses for them and so forth, more than I really like *playing* with them," Deirdre said, opening the box and pulling out neatly folded bright scraps

89

of ribbon and lace, along with fragments of satin and cotton and silk. At the bottom of the box were two small bisque dolls, quite old, with china-blue eyes and real hair, one brown and one blond. They were much less sophisticated than the modern "Barbie" dolls and, I thought, much cuter. One wore a blue gingham dress and pinafore; the other, a long, white, silk nightgown.

"I've had them since I was very little—I guess," Deirdre said doubtfully. "This is Madeline and this is Amelia."

"Why did you name them that?"

"I don't know," Deirdre said, and looked troubled. I realized that these dolls must be older than my own childhood; they might have belonged to Martine herself as a child. I came and examined the contents of the biscuit tin. At the very bottom were two or three gorgeously trimmed dolls' costumes, one of which I suddenly recognized as an exact duplicate of the elaborate opera costume worn in the portrait of Martine, downstairs in the lobby. Had a younger, softer Martine duplicated her opera costumes in miniature for her little daughter's dolls? Were Madeline and Amelia the names of operatic heroines?

Deirdre was smoothing out the silks with loving hands, but her eyes were puzzled, evidently searching, again, in her fluid memories. A psychiatrist, I thought for the hundredth time, would find this a rewarding and responsive patient—and why isn't she having treatment? Why is she dumped here with a resident keeper?

Deirdre burst out, her hands suddenly flying to her temples, "Oh, Susan, there's so much I can't remember! Why can't I remember, why can't I *remember?*"

"I don't know, dear," I said carefully; "maybe some day you will."

She went on gripping her temples with frantic hands, until I was seriously afraid she would hurt herself. "Sometimes I think I'll go crazy! I keep wondering and wondering and I—I'm *afraid* to remember, and yet it scares me *not* to remember! Sometimes it feels as if my head would burst into pieces!"

"Don't worry about it, dear. Come on. Would you like to make more dresses for these dolls?"

She nodded. "I'm not allowed to get magazines, but

sometimes I find *her* magazines." She produced a small cache of fashion magazines. "I'd love to wear pretty clothes like these," she said with typical teen-age wistfulness, "but the hairdos look awfully silly."

"Yours is much nicer," I agreed.

"I've thought I'd try to copy some of these. I used to sew a lot for my dolls, but I can't find my scissors. Will you help me cut out a dress?"

I was happy to have found something to amuse her, and for the next hour we worked contentedly at the table in the window. Deirdre seemed to have a knack for cutting neat dress patterns and she was contentedly stitching a seam in a minute brocade-silk skirt, when a soft knock came at the door. Expecting Carla with lunch, or Mrs. Meadows with a message, I opened it to find Martine McLeod standing there.

She stepped past me into the room without invitation and stood surveying her daughter. Deirdre looked up once, quickly, with dismay, then suddenly swept her work together in her lap, pitifully, as if trying to protect it.

"Playing with dolls—at *your* age!" Martine said scornfully. "Such trash!"

Her contemptuous hand swept the small green skirt to the floor. I watched, appalled, as Deirdre's hand flew to her mouth and she bit at it; then, suddenly, shrieking, Deirdre huddled into herself and crouched down. She crawled under the table and huddled there, sobbing wildly.

In consternation, I stepped forward. "Mrs. McLeod!" I said, in honest shock, "how *could* you? Can't you see that you've only upset her?"

"And I don't think she should be allowed to play with scissors and needles," Martine went on, turning angrily to me. "She might put her eyes out with them."

Suddenly I felt real, honest rage boiling up in me. I kept my voice quiet and courteous, but I spoke with all the authority of a professional nurse, simmering over a hard boil.

"Really, Mrs. McLeod, I insist that you must not come here like this. I'm willing to discuss this later, but at the moment—"

91

"Are you trying to tell me I can't even see my own daughter?"

I felt like retorting, if this is the way you treat your own daughter, God help everyone else. And when have you treated her like a daughter, if it comes to that?

Instead I faced her, my mouth set and rigid, and demanded, "Are *you* trying to tell *me* how to handle *my patient*, Mrs. McLeod? I don't want to offend you, but I *am* in charge here, and I really must ask you to leave."

Firmly, but irresistibly, I stepped forward, edging her backward toward the door, forcing her to step back or lean backward, got her out into the hall, and closed the door behind me; then I said in a soft, furious voice, "Mrs. McLeod, when I was engaged, I was given authority to deal with my patient, and I resent this slander on my professional competence. Now: I *insist*, first of all, that you must not discuss Deirdre in her presence as if she were deaf and dumb. You know very well that she understands everything you say, and it seems that you *try* to upset her." I produced scissors and needle from my pocket, where I had deftly whipped them before leaving Deirdre, and said, "You needn't be afraid that I will allow any patient of mine to handle sharp instruments unless I absolutely trust her with them— though as far as I can tell, Deirdre is perfectly trustworthy. Furthermore"—I was building up a good mad now— "Deirdre does not have these tantrums unless someone upsets her. In the future, if you want to visit her, I insist— I absolutely insist—that you let me prepare her properly, that you try not to upset her, and that you refrain from criticizing her without any reason!" I felt my cheeks absolutely flaming with rage. "If you object to Deirdre's childish choice of pastimes, why don't you provide some more adult amusements for her?"

At that moment Martine looked madder than Deirdre at her worst. Her face was crimson and looked congested with wrath, and her eyes blazed with fury. I turned my back on her.

"Now I must get back to my patient," I said. I swept inside the room, slammed the door in Martine's face, and locked it, mentally bracing myself to cope with another of Deirdre's fits of sobbing and shrieking and hysterical terror. But to my amazement, when I turned from locking the door, Deirdre was kneeling upright by the table. There were tears on her face, and her frail body was still shaken by intermittent spasms of sobbing, but she was not huddled in mortal terror under the table.

"She really won't come in here?"

"She won't," I promised.

Deirdre pulled herself to her feet, then suddenly flew to me and flung her thin arms around my neck. Startled, I hugged her, doll and all, as she whispered, still shaken by sobs, "Oh, if only somebody would make her . . . I never saw anybody stand up to her before! Never! Never!" She was almost babbling with relief. "And you're not afraid of her?"

"Not at all," I assured her gently; "not at all."

Deirdre drew a long, relaxed sigh and wiped her wet eyes. She pushed back her disheveled fair hair.

"I shouldn't get so scared," she suddenly said. "Why do I get so scared all of a sudden, Susan?"

God, I wish I knew! But all I could answer was, "You weren't so scared this time. Maybe you'll get over it."

"Maybe." Her small, pixie face was drawn as if with mighty effort. She brooded, intense, a taut, small study in concentration, for a moment, then drew a long, shaking sigh.

"Maybe," she said, and bent to pick up her doll's skirt from the floor. "Can I have my needle back, Susan? She always thinks I'll hurt myself, but I'll be careful."

"I know," I said, and sank down, relieved, as Deirdre began to sew again, her fair hair falling around her small, pointed chin, her mouth puckered as she stitched. For the moment the tempest had been averted, but I did not deceive myself into thinking I had heard the last of it.

Not from Martine McLeod.

Chapter
Eight

REPERCUSSIONS were not long in coming. That night, when I had seen Deirdre in bed, I received a message on the house telephone.

"Miss Moore," Lowden's courteous voice told me, "Mr. McLeod would like to see you if it is convenient."

I assured him I would be right down and quickly combed my hair before the mirror, but I felt inwardly a little scared. I was growing fond of Deirdre, and now, for the pleasure of telling off Martine, I had jeopardized my position here—for I had no doubt whatever that Mr. Alexander McLeod had been informed of my insubordination. The old gentleman didn't look like the kind to take any back talk from the hired help.

Then I stiffened my backbone. Hired help be damned! These people had got themselves a trained professional—and they could damned well take her advice or buy themselves a tame robot who would do as she was told. They seemed to *want* the girl treated like a congenital idiot! If it came to telling off, I would do a little of it myself! I walked down the stairs with my head high.

The library was dim; over the grand piano the portrait of a younger Martine seemed to draw all the light in the room, and for a moment, looking for the wheelchair of old Mr. McLeod, I did not realize that it was Brant who stood by the mantelpiece, one arm leaning against it, looking past me to Martine, severe in her dark dress, in the shadows.

He drew a long sigh as I came in. A weary, harried sigh. "Well, Miss Moore," he said, in that harsh voice, "would you kindly tell me just what all the racket seems to be about?"

94

Were they lined up to sit in judgment on me? I came forward, facing them squarely.

"Mr. McLeod, one thing should be clearly understood. I am a licensed psychiatric nurse, not a maid or a nursery governess. When I am placed in charge of a private patient, I usually assume it is because I know more about the care of such a patient than the average layman. I doubt if you would hire a lawyer and proceed to argue your own case in court, or a doctor, and operate on your own appendix. If I offended Mrs. McLeod, I am sincerely sorry; but my first loyalty is to my patient, and anything that upsets her is something I have to stop at once. That is no more than my duty."

There was a brief silence in the room—a stunned silence, it felt like. With something like contempt, I thought, *These people are accustomed to saying "Boo" and having everybody jump. It probably shocks them right out of their fancy skins to have someone stand up to them!*

Brant McLeod said at last, thoughtfully, "You know, Martine, there's something in that. It hardly makes sense to get a top-quality professional nurse, and then try to do better ourselves. Miss Moore's got a point. Shows her duty to Deirdre and all that."

Martine said, shaking with rage, "She almost threw me bodily out of the room!"

Was I mistaken, or did his glance rest on her with open skepticism? "Manhandled you, you mean? Actually struck or pushed you?"

"Mr. McLeod, I did not lay a hand on her. It is true that I edged her out of the room in a hurry; Deirdre was upset, and I was afraid she would go into one of her screaming fits."

"Well, she didn't actually *shove* me . . ." Martine said sullenly.

"Look here, Marty," Brant said, "Let Miss Moore tell it?"

I stated succinctly what had happened. When I had finished, Brant's eyes rested on me.

"Sounds all right to me," he said. "I don't see where you have a kick coming, Martine."

"I—are you going to let this—this—"

95

"This person who appears able to handle your daughter," said Brant, suddenly turning on her, his jawline set and rigid. "Deirdre hasn't had a major fit since Susan came. She swims and walks and writes in her bird books and she hasn't *had* a tantrum of any importance. Now, for God's sake, do you want to go back to somebody like Miss Fiske, and have Deirdre hiding in the closet from morning till night and screaming and throwing hairbrushes through the window? By God, I sometimes think you do!" He took one brutal step forward, and Martine actually shrank before him. "Susan's doing a damned good job with Deedee, and I'm not going to have these nasty little nitpicking women's fights wrecking it!"

"Brant, that's not fair. . . ." Martine's beautiful voice was husky, and Brant's face, crossed by the strange shadows, twisted as if in pain.

"Sorry, Martine. I—I didn't mean to hurt you." He swallowed and took another step toward her, and I felt it discreet to cough slightly. Brant turned toward me with a mixture of irritation and impatience.

"Well, then, Miss Moore? I hope you have no complaints? That will do, then. You can get back to your patient, if you're willing, and I'll guarantee there'll be no more trouble."

Quite obviously he had forgotten my existence again, and I went out. What went on between Brant McLeod and his far-too-young stepmother was none of my business, I told myself; but as I went up the stairs I heard, behind the closed door, a soft sound like a woman sobbing—or sighing? At least I had surmounted the challenge to my authority, and Martine would not venture to upset Deirdre again.

As I went upstairs I had high hopes. Without these perpetual upsets, Deirdre might grow stronger and begin to recover. Perhaps I could induce Brant, since he seemed concerned about her, to try treatment again. I was filled with hope and with a soft glow of pride in how well I had handled the situation.

It was the pride that goes before a fall.

96

Chapter
Nine

I woke that night with a strange, almost alarming thought. Deirdre's tantrums seemed to be triggered off by fear. . . . And why should Martine, knowing as well she did what their effect would be, *try* to trigger them off?

It almost seemed as if she *wanted* me to believe the girl madder than she was—and then, there was this business of no treatment, of allowing the girl to drift. . . .

I told myself that I was making up goblins to frighten myself. Why, in the name of God, would anyone *want* to prove a girl of sixteen insane? Why would anyone work upon a child to drive her mad?

Anyone who works around a mental hospital has heard rumors. The famous husband who has his wife shut up in a mental hospital so that he can carry on with a conveniently hired "housekeeper" in her place, without the scandal of a divorce. The rich man whose greedy relations have him shut up to control his fortune.

Those old stories?

But they did happen, I reminded myself. They really happened. I could have named names. The nurses all knew, for instance, that a certain gentle, vague little woman was no more insane than I was—or hadn't been, until a series of shock treatments had confused her memory. And just before I left the state hospital where I had had my final training, there had been a widespread scandal about families who used the place as a dumping ground for their unwanted mothers-in-law rather than having them decently cared for in an old people's home; if an old man or woman grew forgetful or vague, it was cheaper to have them committed to the insane asylum—at public expense—than to look after them at home or pay a trained nurse to do it.

The most harmless senile eccentricities were used as "evidence" of insanity.

But—a girl of sixteen?

These people were millionaires. If Deirdre were heiress to a great fortune . . . ?

I told myself to stop making up soap-opera plots, but I could not stop myself. If the girl's mental incompetence were established from childhood, then when she came of age, who would manage that fortune? A thwarted, restless woman, her guardian.

But that would make them monsters!

People who do things like that are monsters, I retorted to myself, *but they do exist. Remember the children you've seen in hospitals, beaten up or burned or raped by their own parents. Not always poor slum children, either. This is just a little more subtly cruel than that. And do you really believe Martine McLeod incapable of that?*

And I was surprised to hear my own voice answering, *I don't believe that woman's incapable of* anything!

The three-day storm abated, and Deirdre, to her immense delight, could swim again and walk in the woods; the dolls went back into their biscuit tin, and the binoculars and field charts came out again. Deirdre and little Jeremy romped on the beach in the afternoon, with the enormous, shaggy Thumbelina. I watched them carefully, conscientiously, but at the back of my mind, a theory was shaping, slowly.

At the close of one afternoon, when I summoned Deirdre to go into the house, she suddenly flung herself at me.

"Susan, can't Jeremy come and have supper with me? Just this once? I could show him some of my new games. Oh, I miss having him so much!"

I glanced at Hester, and she frowned, doubtful, though Jeremy was clinging to her and begging too.

"Mr. Brant *did* forbid it, Miss Susan."

"Mr. Brant said I was in complete charge of Deirdre," I said, suddenly deciding, "and I'd say it'll be all right."

Jeremy whooped, and Deirdre squealed with joy like a child half her age. The brother and sister hugged each other with delight, and Hester, melting as she looked, still seemed uncertain. "If you'll take the responsibility, Miss Susan . . ."

"I will."

She sighed, relinquishing it with relief. "Then it's as you say. It goes against the grain to part them and say no; indeed it does."

Deirdre's eyes shone electric blue as she dressed for supper that evening, and I reflected, not without a heart-tearing pity, that this was probably the nearest thing to a party that the child had had or attended for years. I wondered when her birthday was and resolved that something should be done about it. In her best frock of pink moiré silk, her hair glossy from the brush, she looked almost her age. In the outside world she would be breathtaking. Would she ever see it?

With all my heart I wished that day would come for her. I had begun to believe that indeed it might come, and sooner than I thought.

Mrs. Meadows, informed of a special occasion, had provided the childrens' favorite foods; Hester and I sat apart at a card table so that they might better enjoy each other's company. I neglected my food, watching with pleasure the interplay of Deirdre's merry chatter with the little boy's queer combination of boisterousness and precocious gravity. I might not like Martine McLeod—I'd been suspecting her of every sin in the Decalogue—but she had certainly given both her children unusual good looks and beautiful manners.

They had finished the chicken and salad and were lingering over the tray of fancy cakes when the explosion came, the moment of stark horror that shook all my self-confidence into rubble. It began innocently, as Jeremy bent to select a fancy cake with pink icing, then drew back. "Would you rather have this one, Deedee?" he asked. "It's the prettiest—and it matches your dress."

She smiled and dimpled. "No, you take it; I like the little ones with chocolate sprinkled things on them."

Jeremy sighed happily. "This is lovely. Like the old days when Margo was with us."

99

I saw Deirdre's face change, the smile wiped off as if by acid. Hester frowned and sat up straight; I felt a curious prickle of fear, without knowing why, that tingling sensation that means that all the little separate hairs on the body are standing on end. I braced myself, without quite knowing why, warned by the old sixth sense I'd acquired on the violent wards of the asylum just before a patient flipped out. . . .

"I liked Margo," Jeremy said mournfully. "Of course I like Susan, too, but why did Margo go away?"

Deirdre's chair went over backward with a crash and the little plate of cream cakes smashed, in a splatter of cream and frosting, to the floor. Deirdre's mouth opened in a sudden, tearing scream; a sound so wild, so agonizing and prolonged, that I thought her small throat would burst. Jeremy sat frozen, his small face white, his mouth agape, a pink-frosted rim still on his upper lip. I was across the room in two steps, but Deirdre backed away from me, still screaming.

"Deirdre . . ." I tried to take her stiff arms, but she thrust me violently away. She was board-stiff, her lips drawn back into the mad mask of tragedy.

"Margo," she screamed, "Margo! *Margo!*"

I held the girl by main force. Jeremy burst suddenly into wild sobs; Hester, crossing the room in a rush, swept her charge into her arms, but Jeremy sobbed and struggled.

"Let go of me! Let go! Deedee, Deedee, what's the matter?"

I tried to calm my shrieking charge with gentle words.

"It's Susan, darling. Hush; hush. I'm right here, and it's all right. . . ."

Deirdre broke away and turned on Jeremy.

"She's *dead,*" she shrieked, "she's dead, lying down with her head all squashed in like an egg—like an egg— and blood all over her face and all over her dress and blood in her hair and blood, blood, blood, and I screamed and tried to shake her and wake her up and she was dead, she was dead, dead, dead, dead, and she came and pulled me off him and shook me and shook me and shook me

100

and he was lying there dead and there was blood all over her dress. . . ."

"Really, Miss!" Hester's shocked, prim voice cut through Deirdre's shrieks and Jeremy's sobs. She held the struggling little boy, her face aglow with righteous rage. "Miss Susan, what a thing for a little boy to have to hear! I hold you responsible, Miss, I do. Never in all my life . . ." words failed her; her eyes blazing, she actually caught up the fighting, sobbing Jeremy in her arms, bodily, and carried him out of the room, slamming the door.

Deirdre's crazy shrieking went on and on; I had lost track by now of the words, which had blended into stammering incoherence. I contented myself with holding the child's hands, afraid Deirdre might do herself an injury with her wildly flailing arms. Again and again I repeated, in low, soothing tones, "There's nothing to be afraid of, Deirdre. It's Susan. I'm right here and you're all right. Don't be frightened."

It seemed hours that I stood there, holding the struggling hands and watching the incoherent, twisting mouth fighting to enunciate words that by now had deteriorated into incoherent, sobbing grunts and syllables; although later I knew that it was rather less than half an hour before the lessening shrieks and sobs muted into long, sighing moans and Deirdre, her whole body seeming to melt and go boneless, sagged forward into my arms. I picked her up like a child and carried her into her bedroom. I could have wept as I gently stripped the crushed, ruined dress from her limp body, took off the pretty pumps and stockings, washed the crimson, streaked face. So much for my theories about a plot to prove Deirdre insane, if the mere mention of her former nurse could touch off this insane raving about blood and death and murder. I felt heartsick with pity. It was like dressing a doll as I slipped her pretty pajamas on her legs and over her head. I put her into her bed and covered her up, surveying the ruins of the party with a heartsick ache.

No wonder Martine had ordered her normal younger child kept away from her demented daughter! The terrified sobs of little Jeremy still seemed loud in my ears.

101

I would always feel responsible. What must it have done to the child, to see his adored, lovely sister disintegrate before his eyes into a raving, shrieking madwoman?

A long sigh from Deirdre brought me swiftly to her side. She whispered, "Susan?"

"I'm here, darling."

She gripped my hand so tightly with her thin fingers that I thought seriously that she would break the bones. "Will she kill you too?"

Sobs began to shake her again, and I said, quickly—anything to humor her—"Nobody will hurt you, or me either. Don't you worry about that. They'd better not try."

"She was lying there dead—and blood on her face . . ."

Had Deirdre actually seen Margo's dead body? Or had this been another of her paranoid fantasies of death, poison, or murder? Every one of her tantrums seemed to revolve around this fear—not that it was an uncommon one with the demented. I said softly, "There's nothing here now. It's all right."

She repeated, with conviction, "I tell you, I saw her lying there dead. . . ."

"Yes, dear; only there's nothing to be afraid of now. Here, I'll stay with you."

"You're like the rest of them," Deirdre said bitterly; "you think I'm crazy; you won't believe me." She turned her back to me and lay staring at the wall, silent and rigid, her fists clenched in hostile rejection.

"Do you want your teddy bear?"

She did not answer. After a very long time, in a small voice, she said, "Yes, please," and when I brought the plush bear and tucked him in beside her, she gripped him with fierce intensity, burying her crimson face in his pale plush fur. She did not speak again, and after a long time I could tell by her quiet breathing that she was asleep.

I sat on, watching her, not wanting to leave her alone. If she should wake in the night, in another fit of shrieking terror, I wanted to be there. I looked at my watch. Nine-thirty. Less than two hours ago, they had been so happy, and I had been so hopeful. And now?

A knock came quietly at the outer door, and I left Deirdre and tiptoed across the floor to open it. Mrs. Meadows stood there, her face, usually so kindly, frozen in hostile anger. She looked past me, grimly, at the ruined cakes on the floor.

"Miss Moore, Mr. Brant wants to see you in the library. Now, at once, if you please."

I demurred. "I don't like to leave Deirdre alone, or with any untrained person——"

She cut through my words. "Mr. Brant says you are to lock her in her room, if necessary, and come immediately to him." She bent and began to gather up the debris, not favoring me with a further look or word.

Reluctantly, I locked Deirdre's bedroom door. I thought that after her fit of crying she would sleep for hours, but I was not going to take the responsibility if she woke and ran away again—or suddenly attacked old Mrs. Meadows! I did not stop to run a comb through my hair or to straighten my rumpled dress. I went swiftly, knowing that if I hesitated I would be afraid to go.

As I opened the library door, it seemed that the distant sobbing of a terrified child still echoed in the corridor. Brant McLeod, standing by the piano, evidently heard it too, for he raised his head, and a look of murderous rage was fixed on me. "Listen to that!" he demanded. "Hester finally had to ask Martine for a sleeping pill for the kid, and it's still going on. Good God, Miss Moore, are you a totally irresponsible fool?"

I opened my mouth to speak, but he swept on, savagely; "I gave orders that the children were not to be allowed to be together, at any time. Those orders have been disobeyed. My father is very much distressed, and he is an old man, and feeble. Would it satisfy you if he had a fatal heart attack, Miss Meddlesome Moore?" He paused, daring me to speak. "Why were my orders—my definite orders—disobeyed?"

Suddenly I was tired of this. I had come down, chastened and apologetic, ready to admit a mistake of judgment and take the consequences. But Brant McLeod's damned arrogance was more than I was going to take.

"What disturbs you more—the fact that two children

103

are in hysterics and your father upset, or that your damned precious 'orders' have been disobeyed?" I demanded.

His face jerked upward, surprised, but I gave him no chance to speak. "Mr. McLeod, I have been very dissatisfied with the handling of this case from the beginning, and now I am being blamed because I have had to work in a blindfold. I asked for Deirdre's history or a consultation with the doctor handling her case. I was given nothing except bland generalities. I asked for instructions and was told to use my judgment. If the girl had broken her leg I would not have known what physician to telephone!" I paused for breath. "You yourself told me to use my own judgment, so I used it. You told me to treat Deirdre with as much freedom as she seemed to deserve, so I obeyed those orders. I'm sick of it," I finished, passionately, "and I completely refuse to go on handling her case at all under these conditions. Please accept my notice at once. I'll stay until you can get someone to replace me—but, believe me, unless this girl is put under the care of a competent psychiatrist at once, the case will be reported —*by me*—to the Department of Public Health!

"Mr. McLeod, any slum child has the chance to be admitted to a free psychiatric clinic, and you, who could afford the best treatment available for Deirdre, are satisfied to have her looked after by a keeper!" I was seething with rage; all my pent-up resentment at this man overflowed. "If you knew how some of those poor people scrimp and save to get even the most casual psychiatric care for their children, and you . . ."

I ran out of words and stood there breathless, too angry to speak. Brant, who had put up a defensive hand, was silent for a moment. At last, with a long sigh, he said, "Miss Moore, I apologize. Will you listen to me?"

An apology? From Brant McLeod? This meant something.

He turned and poured himself a drink from a brandy bottle. He swallowed it, desperately, like a condemned man. I saw his throat muscles working. He said, "Will you have a drink? After tonight, I'm damn sure you could use one."

"Thank you, no. I'm still on duty."

104

"Suit yourself." He sagged, wearily. "Miss Moore, I apologize. It was unforgivable of me to try to keep you in the dark about this. Martine felt that raking up the whole story again would only cause trouble; I argued from the beginning that you should be taken into our confidence, if only for your own safety. Martine said that a psychiatric nurse would be on guard anyhow against violence. I listened to her. I shouldn't have done it." He poured another drink, then dashed it away without tasting it and turned to me with a final, desperate gesture. "I'm trying to put off saying it. I should have told you at first. Deirdre—little, innocent, beautiful Deirdre, that sunny, happy, little girl —Deirdre is a murderess!"

Chapter

Ten

FOR A moment I simply stood and stared at him. The portrait of Martine—beautiful, enigmatic, and malicious—stared down at us; the light caught the untasted brandy in his hand, the polished wood of the piano, glints of metallic threading in the draperies on the wall. I blinked, letting the silence take and echo the incredible word "murderess." I said flatly, "I can't believe it."

"You fool." Brant's voice was not savage now, it was only weary. "She killed Margo Fields."

My knees suddenly went weak. I must have shown it, for he shoved a chair under my knees. "Here. Sit down, damn it."

All I could say was, "But why? Why then is she still at liberty? Why . . . ?"

Brant swallowed hard. "Don't you realize?" he pleaded suddenly, "the poor kid doesn't even know it? Do you know what they'd do to her? Do you *know?* The state hospital for the criminally insane . . . a trial . . . a scandal . . . my father dead of the shock . . . Jeremy's life ruined by having his little sister branded a murderess . ." his voice failed him.

I fought to collect myself. All I could say was, "That explains, then, why some of the people here say that Margo was killed in a fall from the cliffs and others that she drowned."

Brant took a cigar case from his pocket, fiddled with it, and finally asked, "May I smoke?"

His asking recalled me to my senses; an employer does not usually ask his employee, even though she is a lady, for permission to smoke in his own library. I said, "You don't have to ask me, Mr. McLeod."

"Please—Brant," he said, shaking his head slightly. "This damnable business has me nearly out of my mind. . . ."

"Please smoke. I like cigar smoke."

He fiddled with the light. Then he said slowly, "I suppose it's my fault. But I simply could not face what it would do to my family. My family . . . means a lot to me." His gesture included all of Duncarlie Castle. "And Deirdre herself. If the girl had the slightest idea of what she had done or what it could mean to her it would be different. But she hasn't. So I decided we should get someone capable of protecting her, and others, when she goes on these rampages, and"—he made a helpless gesture, "just try to avoid the scandal and trouble."

I asked, "How did you manage? Please tell me the whole story, Mr. McLeod." I shook my head. "I find it hard to believe. The child cries over a hurt bird; I can't *believe* her capable of violence! The other day, when Martine—I'm sorry—when Mrs. McLeod frightened her so terribly, she didn't attack her; she only tried to crawl under the table and hide. I've observed many violent patients, Mr. McLeod"—I remembered—"Brant, rather. They have characteristic patterns. The combative patient attacks; the withdrawing patient withdraws. Deirdre always withdraws."

"I'd give my right arm to be able to believe—" He broke off and shook his head. "All right. I'll tell you.

"We got Margo for Deirdre four years ago—when she was twelve. Before that, we had had a sort of nursery governess for both Jerry and Deedee. You realize Deedee couldn't talk at all. They'd diagnosed complete aphasia. She could hear and understand when we spoke to her, though she had this thing about Martine—I mean, trying to crawl away and hide whenever Martine touched her. She could be taught to dress herself, eat, comb her own hair, sew—but she couldn't talk. Then one day she suddenly said, 'Madeline.' It was the name of a doll she had. She started talking, slowly, but she knew the names of things. Things in the last couple of years, that is; she never remembered anything that happened before she'd lost her voice."

But she remembered her father the other day, I thought suddenly in amazement.

Brant went on, "We thought, 'Perhaps she's coming out of it.' For a while, she was fine; then she began having these violent tantrums of fear again. Margo was—she had been a vocational and speech therapist at a school for retarded children, and we got her as a sort of companion for Deirdre. Lovely girl," he added, his mouth twisting; "exact opposite type from you—I don't mean that the way it sounds; I mean she was tall, dark, slender—willowy, you'd say. Looked a little like Martine must have looked when she was younger, I'd say."

Oh, God! I thought; *if Margo, impatient with her charge, perhaps made some menacing gesture reminiscent of the mother Deirdre seemed to fear and hate so much . . .*

"She worked with Deirdre, got her over her stammering, taught her a lot of things, got her interested in birds and all that, taught her to swim again—Deirdre was afraid of the water when Margo first came, for some reason, and Margo cured her of that fear. She was such a good, gentle girl . . . and Deirdre seemed to love her so much. The same way"—he paused, staring into my eyes fixedly—"as she seems to love you, Miss Moore."

I get the point, I thought; *you don't have to hammer it home.*

"Well. One day Deirdre ran away. We all went looking for her. I took a notion to look on that strip of beach where the sea caves were." He swallowed hard. "I found . . . them." He buried his head in his arms. I sat, waiting. I was numb with horror, yet I knew what was coming. I had heard it all from Deirdre, shrieked out in what sounded like mad raving.

"Margo was lying on the sand with her head crushed," Brant went on. "She must have been dead for more than an hour; she was cold. Deirdre was kneeling above her, almost as rigid and cold as Margo, frozen. She might as well have been dead herself."

"Catatonia?"

"That might be what you call it. And clutched in her hand was a rock. . . ." Brant spoke in a harsh whisper, as if the words were too horrible for utterance. "A rock covered with blood—blood and brains—oh, God, if I live a thousand years I'll never forget!"

He covered his face with his hands and sobbed aloud. A man sobbing is a pitiful sight; the sobs seemed to tear him apart with anguish. "My little sister stark mad, and Margo, with her skull smashed in, like—like an eggshell. I went up to her. I was afraid she'd turn on me, too, but she just knelt there and stared at me as if she'd turned to stone, and then she started to scream. God, those screams; I'll hear them to my dying day. . . ."

"I heard them tonight."

"I took the rock away from her. She let it go like a baby —or a sleepwalker. All I could think of was what it would mean to us all. She didn't even know. She looked up at me so pitifully and said, 'Margo won't wake up; I shook her and she won't wake up.' God forgive me, I . . . I *could not* turn that poor, mad child over to the police and the doctors.

"I made Deedee go over and wash herself in the sea. I—I swam out into the riptide—I didn't give a damn whether I ever got out or not, so of course I did—and I dropped that damned rock into the deepest part of the channel. I led Deedee up to the house and looked poor Margo over. She was all over scratches and bruises—she must have fought like mad, but the scratches looked ambiguous enough so that I decided they *could* have come from falling down the rocks. She *could* have fallen trying to climb the cliffs. Deirdre's evidence wasn't worth anything one way or the other. There was no evidence except what I destroyed.

"I gave my evidence, such as it was, to the state police, leaving out the rock in Deedee's hand. They couldn't question her—they had a police psychiatrist try, but all she'd do was cry and shake and say that Margo wouldn't wake up. They gave her a shot of something, finally, and when she came out of it, she—she'd forgotten the whole thing. She—she asked where Margo was and why Margo didn't come back to put her to bed."

Brant raised his swollen face at last.

"So they gave the verdict as accidental death. They de-

109

cided she must have tried to climb the cliffs and fallen, and that the sight had been such a shock to her mentally disturbed charge that she had gone into hysteria."

"Brant," I said, "*couldn't* it have been that way?"

"With the rock in her hand? Covered with Margo's blood?"

"She might have picked it up—"

Brant spoke bitterly. "I'd give my right arm to believe that. But there's no doubt. She killed Margo, all right. And I should probably be arrested as an accessory after the fact. But for God's sake—would *you* lock up that kid in an asylum for the rest of her life? Are you still going to report us to the Department of Public Health because we don't get a psychiatrist in to probe the whole thing and force her to remember it?

"If you were Deirdre and had *that* to remember—would you *want* to be sane?"

It was silent in the room, so silent that I could hear the ticking of my watch. I felt bruised and exhausted. It was very late. And yet it had been less than half an hour since I had entered this room, and in it, I seemed to have aged half a lifetime of violence and fear. Brant raised pleading eyes to me.

I spoke, almost without thinking. "Brant, if I were you, I'd have done the same thing!"

"God bless you, Susan!" He grasped my hands and drew me to my feet. He stood there, stooped over me, for a moment that was electric in its intensity, and I was aware of the closeness of his sturdy body, the strength in his hands, the faint male smell of his skin. I drew a long sigh. Then the moment passed and he stepped back from me.

"Then—you'll stay with Deirdre?"

"I will."

"And you'll take care? I mean . . ." He swallowed hard. "It's a ghastly, a God-awful responsibility to give anyone. But if she were in an—an insane asylum, it would be the same responsibility, only to the other patients rather than to her family."

"I can take care of her, yes," I promised. Stunned, I looked at my watch. "Brant, I—I must get back to Deirdre."

He nodded, drawing apart from me. He, too, looked dazed. I went out of the library. The great halls were silent around me, echoing, ringing with my step. These ancient walls had been transported here, stone by stone, and before that how many centuries had they seen, and what violence, madness, and murder? No wonder I had felt the haunted desperateness of the place! Did Martine know? Did old Alexander McLeod know?

And a shocking thought crossed my mind: Did Brant know? *Or had this been a superb piece of acting? And why?*

With a firm, harrowing effort, I shook off the mood of tragedy, bracing myself to professional mannerisms again. I had heard horrible things before this in the asylum; why did this seem so much more horrible? The meek little woman who had one day given cyanide to all five of her little children, offering only as excuse, "The Virgin Mary spoke to me and said she wanted them in Heaven." Was it only Deirdre's beauty, the haunted, overcharged atmosphere of the castle, that made the grim story work on my imagination overtime?

I entered Deirdre's playroom, noting peripherally that Mrs. Meadows, or someone else, had cleaned away the remnants of the spilled dinner. I slipped the key into the lock and tiptoed into Deirdre's bedroom.

The night-light cast a soft pink glow over the furniture, the white robe hanging on the bathroom door, the white fur of the teddy bear—the bare empty turned-back white sheets!

Deirdre's bed was empty. . . . She was gone.

The night remaining is the worst in my memory.

I checked and rechecked the lock; yes, it had been locked.

She was not under the bed. She was not in the closet. She was not hiding in the bathroom. The ornamental grilles at the window were undisturbed, and anyway, under the window was a sheer forty-foot drop. For God's sake, had the girl learned how to walk through the walls? Or had she somehow, with the diabolical cunning of the insane, learned to pick a lock with a stolen hairpin, or found or improvised a duplicate key? I searched the rooms, with growing dismay, for my vanished patient, sure that another charge of negligence would be added to my already heavy account—I had been deceived by a falsely innocent face (Martine's phrase!) into thinking her harmless. But where, in God's name, was she hiding? And what was she doing? Finally, with growing despair, I realized it was out of my hands. I picked up the house phone and asked for Brant McLeod.

He received the news with amazing calm. For some reason—perhaps only because we had both worn out our emotions earlier—we managed not to raise an alarm. He dispatched Mrs. Meadows to see, quietly, if Martine was safe—if the girl were hiding in her mother's rooms. He asked Lowden to check old Mr. Alexander's suite without alarming the old man, and rang Hester on the house phone to alert her that Deirdre had run away again, asking her to keep very close watch on Jeremy.

We met in the lower hall; I began to blame myself, but he cut me short. "Forget it. We haven't watched her closely enough. I'll have the lock changed, and you'll have to carry the key around your neck. The thing now is to find her. If she's simply hiding in the castle . . ." He shrugged. "There are almost eighty rooms; we'll just have to start searching. She might find something and hurt herself . . . that's what I'm most afraid of. Or she might have run away outside in the dark . . . in which case she might fall into the sea, or over the rocks. We'll have to get the servants up and start them searching; but I'd rather not let Martine know."

I nodded. We had enough trouble without Martine's accusations. Somehow we had become conspirators, and through the worry of it, I had the most amazing sense of solidity with Brant. Was it only because we both loved Deirdre? For I realized that I did love my forlorn little charge; loved her as I might have loved a child of my own. I, too, was ready to risk my own safety and reputation to protect her and let her live out her life happily without the memory of her act of madness.

If she had done it! . . .

112

Even if she hadn't, her evidence could never be taken. Brant's account of the matter would mean loss of liberty forever for Deirdre; the evidence was six months gone in the riptide, never to be recovered, and if Brant, in shock, had been mistaken, no one would ever know. Certainly not Deirdre.

I was willing to give her the benefit of the doubt. I knew violent patients; Brant did not. If Deirdre was violent—I myself was mad.

I searched all that night, calling, looking at all her favorite bird haunts, knowing that I might pass her in the darkness a hundred times and never know it, if she wanted to hide from me. My face and hands were torn with bramble scratches, my ears echoing with the cries of strange nightbirds and the never-ending wash of the sea on the rocks. At last, as the gray light began to redden into dawn, I sat down on a rock, realizing wearily what must be done. A real search must be organized, by daylight. The shore must be searched, too. And—reluctantly I came to the conclusion—the police must now be notified.

Far away, through the faint lightening of birdsong, I heard Brant's voice, hoarsely, hopelessly, still calling, "Deedee! Deedee!"

A harsh barking boomed at my feet; the huge clumsy Thumbelina bounced and wagged around my knees, pulling and grabbing at my shoes. Absently, I patted her, waiting for the enthusiasm of her greeting to subside.

"Woof! Woof! Woof!"

"Yes, yes, Thumbie!" I said, impatiently, "Down! Good girl, now! Down! You're no help at all. If you could find Deirdre, now . . ."

The dog clearly lifted her ears at Deirdre's name; she woofed loudly, licked my muddy shoe with a slobbery tongue, then gently seized my shoestring in her teeth, pulling and worrying at it. I had never known Thumbelina to act like this before! Did she . . . Was it possible that the dog could lead me to Deirdre?

"Find Deirdre, Thumbie," I said, through growing excitement; "Find Deirdre!"

I stood up. The dog woofed hard again and set off at a

113

bound. I followed; she stopped, looked back intelligently, and when she saw that I followed, lolloped off toward the shore.

I clambered up the steep slope—for Thumbelina had never heard of a path—puffing a little with effort; then I stopped in disgust; Thumbelina was leading me to the beach with the sea caves. For goodness' sake, the dog had simply wanted a romp to her favorite haunt. That was what came of trying to impute sanity to Deirdre and intelligence to a Newfoundland dog!

"No, Thumbie," I said firmly; "down, girl!"

Deirdre would never come here. She was terrified of the place. *And with good reason?*

Thumbelina stopped and whined. She tried to drag me on. I pushed her away, then stopped, frozen.

In the wet, muddy sand, I saw the print of a small, naked foot.

I shouted. I started to run down the path leading to the rocky, dangerous beach. The tide was coming in, and the beach was narrowing fast, every wave licking away a little more of the sand. I yelled frantically for Brant and pelted down to the beach, shouting Deirdre's name.

The strip of beach was empty, but a small trail of naked footprints led across the wet sand to the sea caves. There, at last, shadowed by the overhang of the dark cliff, I found her kneeling in the sand, the rags of her pink gingham pajamas hanging around her pale, cold little body.

I approached her carefully, afraid she might take fright and bolt; if I had to struggle with her, the incoming tide might trap us here before I could summon help or get her to the path.

But as I approached, my foot crunched a shell. She started, as if waking from a deep dream, and rose swiftly to her feet. She backed away.

"Deirdre, it's Susan, darling," I said gently, trying not to remember that this girl, less than six months ago, had attacked and killed a beloved nurse—*or had she?* I cast a swift look at her hands, but they hung, open and empty and harmless, at her side. I approached closer, warily. Now. Now I could spring at her and grab her. . . .

She said, in her ordinary voice, "What on earth are you looking at me like that for, Susan?"

I found my own voice and said, "And what, may I ask, are you doing out here at this hour of the night—or morning?"

She glanced down indifferently at the rags of her pajamas. She said, "I got scared. I ran." She came toward me and put her hand confidingly in mine; warily, but with growing confidence, I seized it in mine. Her eyes were clear, free of the maddened fear.

I said, with heartfelt relief, "Let's get you home, honey."

She nodded, shivering a little. "It's cold, and I don't like it here." She wet her lips with her tiny pink tongue. "This is—this is where people die. I had to know if—if I really would die if I came here."

I made my voice hearty and practical—anything not to alarm or argue with her. "Well, you're not dead and neither am I, but we're going to have salt water for breakfast unless we get going, little girl. Come on; let's go." I had exhausted all my surprise by now; it did not even seem strange to me that Deirdre had come here, where nothing could force her to go a month ago. She was docile as I led her up the path, stopping briefly to put my own coat around her ruined pajamas. She sighed gratefully at the warmth. I warned her not to step on the sharp rocks, but she picked her way carefully.

The waves were racing in, now, and the surf was pounding wildly. One wave rolled shallowly across the beach to the very foot of the cliff, and I urged Deirdre along, breathing a brief prayer of thanks that I had followed Thumbelina's lead. She could have been trapped here by the tide and drowned and swept out to sea. And we would never have known.

She drooped like a sick, weary child as we climbed the path. "I'm so tired. So tired, Susan. And this is where people die. They died here. I found her here, you know. With blood all over her face. . . ."

"I know, dear. I know. Don't worry about it now."

"She killed her. Like the other time. There were rocks coming down and down. I hid under the cliff. And Margo

115

fell down and couldn't get up. . . ." She clung to me, shivering violently, but I was not listening. I shouted to Brant, and after a moment I heard his swift steps crashing through the underbrush.

He clasped Deirdre, wet pajamas, bulky coat, and all, in his arms. She sagged forward; she had fainted. Brant picked the lifeless girl up in his arms, and we walked toward the castle through the morning birdsong, weary, wet, filthy and exhausted, with Thumbelina romping around us in triumphant circles and her barks scaring the birds from the trees.

Chapter

Eleven

WE GOT Deirdre into the house, and Brant laid her on her bed: I made a mental note to search the room again—and Deirdre's clothes and belongings—for the duplicate key. If the girl could escape from a supposedly locked room . . . Then I remembered Brant's promise to have the lock changed. I reminded him of it, and he said, "Yes. I'll have it attended to today. . . . I think she's coming round."

Deirdre opened her eyes. They looked immense, dark, and bruised in her pale face, a face streaked with sea-water, dirt, and tears. She surveyed us without question or surprise. I said soothingly, "It's all right, dear. Go to sleep, now; you've been up all night."

"I'm not sleepy." She caught my hand with an agitated grip. "Susan, there's something I have to tell you, something awful—"

"Not now, Deirdre. Please." I turned to Brant, saying, "You'd better go. I'll undress her and get her cleaned up a little, and by that time she'll probably be sleepy. You might ask them to send up some breakfast, too."

"But what about you, Susan? You look completely done up," Brant said, and I suddenly became conscious of my skirt and blouse, muddy, stained, torn by the briers and the rocks, my dirty face and muddy shoes and damp hair, hanging in lank, sea-wet strands.

I flushed awkwardly. "Oh, a bath and fresh clothes will put me right again."

"But you've been up all night, Susan!"

"No matter," I said, lowering my voice; "when Deirdre's asleep perhaps I can catch a nap, but I'd better stay with her for the present."

He moved toward the door, beckoning me to follow; I gently loosed Deirdre's clutching fingers from mine and moved outside the door. He said in an urgent undertone, "She might start crying and shrieking again. Listen. . . ." He paused, and through the opened door I heard Deirdre's sobs break out once more.

I said, "She'll cry herself to sleep in a while. She's been up all night too, remember."

"But suppose she doesn't? Listen," Brant said, "I'm going to get one of Martine's sleeping pills for her. They can't be very strong; her doctor gives them to her by the dozen. But that means Deirdre will get some sleep and you can, too."

I should have protested. I didn't know the exact composition and strength of the pills. But I did remember that Hester had given little Jeremy one of them, so they were probably some harmless bromide or barbiturate preparation, not especially strong. I said, "All right, but I may not be able to get her to take it; when she gets in one of her fits, she has the idea that people are trying to poison her."

Brant shrugged. "Drop it in her cocoa, then. No, Susan; you need sleep, or you'll never be able to cope with the girl."

"All right," I said at last, "I'll do that." Deirdre's sobs were growing anguished, and she was calling my name; I turned away from Brant and hurried back to her. She was lying there sobbing helplessly and trying to speak. I soothed her, stripped off the remnants of torn pink pajamas—they would hardly have served for dustcloths now—and got her under a warm shower, where I scrubbed the salt water from her, toweled her dry, and dressed her in warm flannel pajamas. She submitted to these ministrations passively, without protest, still shaking now and then with sobs. I did not talk; I was afraid some chance word might set off another fit of shrieks or wild weeping. By the time I had her tucked in with her teddy bear, Brant rapped at the door, a tray in hand.

"I brought it up," he said, then lowered his voice. "There's a sleeping pill in the cocoa. Get her to drink that, and she'll be dead to the world in twenty minutes. Then you can sleep a few hours, at least, without any trouble."

I nodded gratefully and took the tray back. Deirdre only nibbled at a piece of toast, but she drank the hot cocoa with thirsty haste and asked for more. Soon, as Brant had predicted, her lashes began to droop over the sea-blue eyes, and she snuggled her head sleepily against the teddy bear.

"So tired . . . when I wake up, Susan, I want to tell you something . . . something I just remembered. . . . I keep wondering why I didn't realize it before . . . about Margo . . ."

Her voice trailed off; she was fast asleep, her breathing deep and slow and quiet. I surveyed her with relief. *When she wakes up,* I thought, *she'll have forgotten it all again. And if she sleeps for a few hours, I'll have time to find that damned key she must have hidden somewhere.*

I was not sleepy at all, although the thought of a bath and breakfast and fresh clothes was heavenly. I had stayed up all night more than once before this, and I knew infallibly what my reaction was. After the initial weariness, there came a sort of second wind, when I couldn't sleep even if I wanted to and that was all there was to it. It wore off in six or eight hours, so by about four-thirty this afternoon, I was going to feel half-dead again. But the spurt of nervous energy was strong in me now. I'd change my clothes and eat something—some good hot coffee would be marvelous—and then, while Deirdre was safely asleep, I'd take the room apart, if I had to, hunting for her concealed key.

I went back to my room, to find Carla there with a breakfast tray. "Mr. Brant said to bring your breakfast here," she said, "because of Miss Deirdre being asleep." She looked with frank curiosity at my ruined dress and shoes.

I said, "Breakfast is fine, but I think I'll have a bath first—no, damn it, it will all be cold."

Carla said, "I'll run your bath, Miss, while you eat, if you like."

"Thanks." I sank down gratefully on the edge of the bed, reaching for the hot-dish cover. Scrambled eggs and bacon, sliced fresh peaches, hot buttered toast, and a small pot which, when I poured it, yielded not the fresh hot coffee I expected, but a rich, brown stream. I frowned at it. "Carla, where's my coffee?"

She came to the bathroom door, her head poking out through a halo of steam. "Mr. Brant said to bring you this, same as he fixed for Miss Deirdre. He said he expected you'd be wanting to sleep, and coffee would keep you awake."

Damn. And I'd wanted some coffee. I frowned, and Carla said, "I can go down and fix you some coffee, if you'd rather, Miss Moore."

Oh, the hell with it. "Maybe later," I said; "right now anything hot will be all right." I began to sip the cocoa—it was too sweet, but at least it was hot—and anyhow, didn't chocolate contain a stimulant, too? Theobromine or something like that. It was mostly suggestion, anyhow. I remembered a bridge-playing friend of mine whose husband had, without her knowledge, substituted decaffeinized Sanka for her regular coffee. She had gone on drinking cup after cup, "To keep her awake," and sleeping no more than usual. I also knew a man whose last nightly act had always been to drink a cup of hot coffee. He said it helped him sleep. I stuck a fork into the scrambled eggs.

I had cleaned up the tray and finished a second cup of chocolate by the time I was ready for my bath. I threw my ruined skirt and blouse into the hamper and stepped gratefully into the water. It was perfectly right, warm but not hot, and scented with pine essence. It felt wonderfully soothing, and I slid down full length, with only my head out of the water, relaxing with a luxurious sigh. Deirdre was asleep, so I could enjoy a nice, long soak.

But what a night it had been, and what a narrow escape! If Thumbelina had not led me to the sea caves, I'd never have thought of looking there. I must remember to tell Hester about that. Jeremy might follow his big dog down there for a romp and get cut off by the tide. Thumbelina evidently loved the place, for the other day when Brant had shown me the sea cave, she had been there. Brant had kissed me that day. Last night I had almost thought he would kiss me again . . . my mind wandered. Drowsily I slid downward. I hoped Hester wouldn't be too angry about last night; she was a nice girl. Jeremy was a nice little boy. It was too bad . . .

I splashed suddenly awake with my eyes and nose full of bath water and sat upright, shaking my head to clear it. What on earth was the matter with me? I was never sleepy after a night out. I hauled myself wearily out of the tub. I felt so sleepy. It would be good to lie down. Just for a minute, then I'd have to find that damned key. Just for a minute. . . . I moved, with groping feet, toward the bed . . . just to lie down and sleep. . . .

A sudden, shocking thought flashed through my already groggy mind.

I'm never sleepy like this; you'd think I was doped. Did the chocolate get mixed up, and did I get the sleeping pill meant for Deirdre?

I shook my head, dazed. If I had, that meant that Deirdre hadn't had one . . . she might wake up and cry for me . . . I couldn't go to sleep. She might be awake and crying for me at this moment. . . .

Groggily, I sat upright and put my hands to my head. A sentence from the textbooks in nursing school flashed across my mind, that there were very few sedatives, and almost none which could be given by mouth, which can put someone to sleep if he resists them strongly enough. I blinked my eyes savagely a few times, groped my way to the bathroom, and splashed cold water on my face; then, deliberately, I turned the shower on full, ice cold, and stood under it for a minute or two.

Whew! Fatigue mixed with even a mild sleeping pill— but even so, I couldn't dare to sleep; Deirdre wasn't even locked in her room. A disturbed patient in a fit of violence will sleep very fitfully; she might already be awake. Hastily, I dressed in a clean skirt and blouse and hurried down the hall to her room.

Deirdre lay as I had left her, silent, her face pale. Her breathing was slow and deep . . . and a little too loud. Suddenly, with a spasm of fear, I bent over her and touched her hand. It was icy cold, and her pulse, when I found it, was slow and irregular.

What, in God's name, had happened?

Sleeping pills. And I had no idea what kind they were

or how strong. I must have been out of my mind, blurred by fatigue, to let Brant simply get some anonymous sleeping pill and ladle it out to my patient. Not knowing the strength, not knowing even the kind . . . whether morphine or barbiturate! And Deirdre, although sixteen, was frail. . . .

I picked up the house telephone. "Mrs. Meadows," I said urgently, "get hot coffee up here—strong, black coffee, and some more blankets—plenty of blankets—and a hot-water bottle. Then get me Mrs. McLeod—I don't give a damn if she *is* still sleeping, I don't care if she never gets up before noon, get her up here!" I hung up and turned back to Deirdre, my mind awhirl. Then she must have had the sleeping pill after all, and I had just succumbed to a completely untypical streak of fatigue—but how lucky it was! Otherwise, sure Deirdre was asleep, I might have slept in my room for hours, and Deirdre . . .

"Dead to the world in twenty minutes," Brand had said.

Dead—to the world. And to all of us!

Frantically, I sought again for the faint, irregular thread of pulse. I began to slap her face softly. She moaned almost imperceptibly, but did not move. I got a washcloth, wet it in icy water, and began to sponge her face; even this did not bring any response other than the faint moan. The door opened, and Mrs. Meadows entered, laden with blankets and a hot-water bottle; behind her were Martine McLeod—and Brant.

I said to Mrs. Meadows, "Fill that bottle—boiling hot. And give me the coffee." I turned to Martine, urgently. "What are your sleeping pills? What strength? What kind?"

"Sleeping pills?" She looked at me, frowning. "Miss Moore, have you lost your wits? I don't know. Something the doctor gave me." She rubbed her eyes. "I'm still half-asleep. Brant, what is this insanity?"

Brant said roughly, "Martine, can't you get it through your head this is serious?"

"But what is all this about sleeping pills? How would *Deirdre* get one of my sleeping pills?" Martine looked down at her prostrate daughter in confusion.

Martine was wearing a deep-crimson velvet house robe

122

which was amazingly like the crimson robe of the painting downstairs, and the contrast between her haggard face and the glowing beauty, even at that moment, was sharp and shocking.

Brant said, "I knew you were sleepy, but what the hell! I came to your door this morning . . ."

Martine rubbed her eyes. She said, "I remember. At some ungodly hour, and said Miss Moore wanted a sleeping pill. I was only about half-awake; I handed you the bottle. What did you with it?"

I said quickly, "How strong were they? Brant, how many did you put in the cocoa?"

"One," Brant said, frowning, "The rest are down in my coat pocket where I left them, I think. Martine, how strong are those damned things? Would one of them knock out a kid Deirdre's age?"

"I don't know," Martine said; "I thought it was for Miss Moore; I never thought it was for Deirdre. I was half-asleep. I don't know what they are."

I thought it was time to break in on this. "Then get your doctor on the telephone, Mrs. McLeod. Find out *immediately* exactly what they are and how many grains they are. Of course, people differ in their reactions to drugs—Demerol, Seconal, anything like that. If they happened to be something like strong Nembutal—" I broke off. "And you, Brant. Go and get the pills; I may be able to tell what they are by looking at them."

I busied myself trying to force the hot coffee down Deirdre's throat. It was very strong and black, and I found myself hoping desperately that this—the standard treatment for barbiturate overdosage—was *not,* as I had told myself desperately, mere suggestion. When Brant returned with the sleeping-pill bottle, I looked at it in horror.

"These are three-grain Seconal," I said; "nothing I'd give a child in a thouand years! For God's sake, Mrs. McLeod, do you realize these are almost the strongest sleeping pills made?" I turned on Brant, fiercely. "You told me they were the same as Hester had given Jeremy!"

Martine was white, but her face was unbending. "I thought it was you who wanted them, Miss Moore," she said. "If you wanted the ones that our doctor gave me for

123

Jeremy—he has occasional nightmares—you might have thought to ask Hester."

She turned angrily on Brant. "You knew I was half-asleep. What did you do—decide one wasn't enough, and give her two or three?"

I was shocked at this sudden altercation. "That can all wait till later," I said, bending over Deirdre again, "but I want a doctor here. As soon as you can get him."

Martine's face went white. "More scandal? More talk?"

"Doctors don't gossip," I said harshly. "Would you rather have Deirdre dead? I can't undertake to handle barbiturate poisoning unless I'm absolutely sure what she's had and how it affects her."

Brant said, "Could *one* pill kill her? Just one?"

"If I was sure she'd only had one . . . If I was sure that she's not allergic to all barbiturates as some people are . . ."

Brant said, with a rough, silencing gesture at Martine, "Shut up, Martine. This is serious. I'll call Mason. He knows the family and he'll keep his mouth shut." He strode out. I was still rubbing Deirdre's cold hands and feet, trying to get her to swallow the hot coffee, anxiously feeling her pulse. I never knew when Martine went out. I had managed to rouse Deirdre a little, and I was walking her up and down the room, through her sleepy protests, when at last the door opened and a fat, bald little man with the unmistakable air of a medical man came in.

"Nurse? I'm Doctor Mason. Now just what has happened?" Even as he spoke, he was fumbling for his stethoscope. I got Deirdre on the bed again, opening her pajama top.

He listened briefly to my account, then nodded. "You did the right thing. Heart's all right, pulse almost normal by now, temperature almost normal I'd say. Safe to just let her sleep the rest of it off, if you want to, though I'll stick around an hour or so in case she has any relapse or any signs of heart failure. Watch her carefully; take her pulse every ten minutes and call me if it shows any signs of failing." He glowered at me. "Very irresponsible conduct, Miss Moore; you could lose your license over this."

124

I bent my head; it was true. Letting someone else give anonymous sleeping pills to a patient in my charge was inexcusable. I could only plead fatigue, the letdown after a night of ghastly fear.

"See here," Brant said from the door; "if anyone's to blame, it's me, not Susan. I knew Marty had some sleeping pills she gives little Jeremy—"

Martine broke in, furiously, behind him, "Then you should have said *those!* You said *my* sleeping pills!"

"I did," Brant said angrily, "if you were half-asleep . . . that's a hell of an unnatural mother! Did you know we spent all night looking for the kid all over the God-damned island?"

Dr. Mason said, "I know the pills Mr. McLeod means; they are a pediatric prescription—quarter-grain phenobarbital. You could have given this little girl four or five of them, and she wouldn't be in this state." He frowned. "Offhand I'd say she'd had about six grains of Seconal, which could be a dangerous overdose. But then, anyone as fragile as she is, I'd hesitate to give her even two grains of Seconal."

Martine said, "I still think Brant thought they were Jerry's pills and gave her two or three by mistake!"

"Damn it, I didn't! What are you trying to pull, Martine?" He seized her wrist, roughly.

Deirdre moaned at the sound of her mother's voice, and Dr. Mason said, "Out of here, all of you! Irresponsible idiots . . . messing around with sleeping pills as if they were candy!" He followed them out, still muttering angrily. "And keep your voices down! If old Mr. McLeod gets any hint of this . . . you know, Mrs. McLeod, that your husband can pop off any minute at a shock, and I happen to know he's fond of this child."

Then, I thought as they left me alone with Deirdre, *he seems to be the only one. Martine seems a lot more concerned with proving she hasn't done anything wrong than with whether Deirdre lives or dies. Brant . . .* Goose pimples suddenly ran down my spine.

Had he, perhaps, administered the overdose—*on purpose?*

Had I, perhaps, actually *had* a sleeping pill, too—just

125

to make sure I *wouldn't* wake up until Deirdre was safely "dead to the world"?

But what purpose could he possibly have had?

His anguished confession last night, of concealing evidence that Deirdre had done a murder . . .

A confession that the poor demented child could never prove or disprove! And what she blurted out in her ravings . . .

I shook my head to clear it. *Susan*, I thought, *you're getting affected by this nuthouse, too. First you suspect Martine of poisoning the kid or trying to scare her into insanity; now you suspect Brant of murder—murder at least twice—just because of a perfectly natural misunderstanding between two kinds of pills. The befuddled Martine, half-asleep when wakened at five thirty, might very well have misunderstood Brant's story and, thinking that I wanted the sleeping pills, given him her own rather than the pediatric prescription in her care for Jeremy. Brant just might*—the ignorance of laymen about sleeping pills was ghastly—*have decided that if one sleeping pill was good for Jeremy, Deirdre, being twice his age, would need two. And then, realizing his terrifying mistake, denied it. The important thing*—I checked Deirdre's pulse again and found to my gasping relief that it was normal—*is that Deirdre is all right.*

Dr. Mason came back when I was, at last, relaxing and sipping a cup of the coffee. "Well, it's a miserable business, but fortunately no harm done, Nurse," he said. "The girl must have a strong heart. Careless of her mother and stepbrother, of course, but McLeod explained how it had happened, and laymen *do* things like that."

I said, "I should have examined the pills first."

"You should," he agreed, "but since no harm was done this time . . . He told me you'd been up all night. I can understand how it happened, Nurse, but be more careful from now on.

"The girl isn't usually my patient," he went on. "I gather that Robertson, the little boy's doctor, looks after her; and McLeod tells me there's some sort of psychiatrist.

"Glad to do what I could, of course."

And there the matter rested. But the seed of suspicion,

dropped in my heart during that terrifying morning when Deirdre had lain between life and death, remained.

Did one of them want her dead?

And why?

I continued to wonder as I sat watching the girl sleeping her way back to normal waking—or as near to normal as Deirdre could ever be.

Deirdre slept all the rest of that day. Late in the afternoon, leaving her to Mrs. Meadows, I had a short nap; when I came back she had awakened and was lying curled up, drowsily cuddling her teddy bear; she spooned up some hot soup sleepily and soon dropped off again. I decided I could postpone the search for the key—I'd sleep on the couch in Deirdre's playroom tonight, in case she should try any more unauthorized night ramblings. But I felt that after the day's ordeal, she'd sleep soundly.

It must have been well after eleven when the house telephone rang in the hall outside and went on ringing. Finally, cursing the noise, I padded outside and picked it up, and Brant's voice, urgently, said, "Can you come down to my room, Susan? Bring something with you for a faint; Martine's passed out on me!"

I hurried to my room, collected smelling salts and ammonia, and quietly rapped at Brant's door. He opened it, in his dressing gown, and I stepped back, slightly startled. He said, impatiently. "Come along; she's inside."

I raised a mental eyebrow, but I had suspected something like this all along.

Martine, wearing a fragile gossamer robe, was lying on Brant's turned-down bed. With one swift glance, I realized that this was no faint. Her posture was too composed— and her mouth too set. I lifted her limp wrist and felt, as I had guessed, her pulse ticking as regularly as my own wristwatch. It was a perfect stage faint. I remembered that this woman had been on the stage.

Lovers' quarrel?

Brant said, "She came down here to speak to me about the children—she didn't want to frighten my father, she said, by talking where he could hear. Then she just up and fainted on me." His words were choppy, agitated, and

127

I thought, *Oh, so that's the way the wind lies?* I said calmly, "I wouldn't worry about it, Mr. McLeod. I'll soon bring her around."

There are two or three fairly painful ways of rousing a person even from a real faint—and exposing a malingerer instantly. Pressure on the eyeball is one way; a hard squeeze of a woman's nipple is another. But if Brant was going to play it straight—I crushed the ampul of ammonia in a handkerchief and applied it firmly to Martine's nostrils. She gasped, coughed, choked, and sat up violently, sneezing and furious. Her look at Brant was little short of murderous.

Brant was arrogant and composed. He said, "Did you faint, Martine dear? Your next line is, 'where am I?'"

She put a hand to her head. "Miss Moore? Oh—I must have fainted." I realized that on the stage this woman must have been exceedingly convincing, for after that one murderous glare, she played perfectly the part of the woman who has, embarrassingly, fainted and been revived. "Did Brant call you down?"

"I thought it was best," Brant said smoothly, "as long as we *have* a registered nurse in the house. I didn't want to alarm anyone else." I realized that if it had been, as I suspected, a quarrel or even a compromising situation, Brant had given Martine a convincing cover story that would save her own dignity . . . and his. Had he been deceived by Martine's faint—or not?

I said, "Would you like me to help you back to your own room, Mrs. McLeod?"

"Please." Her voice was faint. She was playing her part well. For me? I gave her my arm. I could tell the difference between a real and a phony swaying of steps. But as the door opened, I recoiled slightly at the sight of old Alexander McLeod, propelling his wheelchair swiftly down the corridor. He rolled hastily on toward us, and his lined face was troubled and angry.

"Martine! Where—"

"It's all right, Father," Brant said quietly, "Martine fainted, but I didn't want to alarm you. Miss Moore brought her around."

He demanded, "What was she doing down here at this hour of the night? Do you people think I'm a complete fool of an old dotard? Damned if I'll be kept in the dark about what goes on in my own house! And if you think you can pull the wool over my eyes, Brant—"

"Father . . . !" he appealed.

"Aleck, you are ridiculous," Martine said sharply. "You know Doctor Mason said you were not to be alarmed; your heart, you know. I wanted to speak to Brant—some tiresome business about Deirdre; the girl is running away again."

Old Mr. Alexander slanted his sharp gray eyebrows at his wife. He said, dryly, "Maternal solicitude comes strangely on your lips, Martine. The roles of Norma or Adelia never suited you, as I can remember. Poor type-casting. You needn't pretend." He glared at her, his breath suddenly coming short.

I said quietly, "Fortunately I carry smelling salts, Mr. McLeod. It's nothing serious."

"Hmmm." He looked at me. "They've even got you . . ." he broke off.

I said, "Mr. McLeod, are you feeling well?" I felt somewhat alarmed. His color was poor, and his breathing rattled in his dry throat. His smile was a mere stretching of the lips, a death's-head grimace. His erect posture seemed sustained by great effort.

The man is dying, I thought. *Dying, and he knows it. A momentary shock could snuff his life out like a candle flame.* The imprint of death was written in large block letters on his forehead. But what was their game? Not that I felt Martine had much love for her husband, but couldn't she wait till the man was cold in his grave? It couldn't be long now—and then, without a qualm, she could take whatever men she wanted. Ross—or, I supposed, Brant, though tongues might wag at a marriage between stepson and stepmother. But they were almost the same age. Or, if Martine were a real bitch, she could have them both.

Or—a suddenly frightening thought—had Martine's acts been coldly calculated, either to shock the old man . . . or *to turn him against his son?* Had she carefully

129

planned to be found in his room—in his bed—and had Brant frustrated her by summoning, quickly, the best chaperon he could find, a trained nurse?

I looked surreptitiously at Brant. He seemed harried, weary, a picture of injured righteousness. He said, "Perhaps, Miss Moore, if you're sure Deirdre is all right alone, you'll help Martine back to her rooms. And I'll stay with Father. Come, Father, I'll wheel the chair; it's a strain for you to wheel yourself. Why didn't you ring up Lowden?"

"And have the whole house gossiping?" the old gentleman asked with asperity. "I'll be all right. Perhaps, Miss Moore, you'd give me a hand? I could use a couple of those smelling salts myself."

Puzzled, I said, "As you like, Mr. McLeod," and began to propel his chair along the corridor.

Martine followed, hovering, anxious; he turned his head harshly and said harshly, "Get to bed, you conniving bitch, and let me alone! Any damned bed you please!"

Martine said, her beautiful voice thrilling with indignation, "Aleck, how can you? You're not yourself tonight," and swept away with a haughty air. He slumped in his chair, tiredly directing me with the merest gesture to his room. When he was there, he allowed me to assist him into his bed. He felt light and dried-out in my arms.

"And now if you'll hand me that glass of water . . ." he thumbed a tablet from his shirt pocket. "Well, Miss Moore, what do you think of my stepdaughter?"

I said, wondering which way this tended, "I'm very fond of Deirdre, sir. With help and psychotherapy, I think the girl might be normal some day . . ." then, remembering Brant's story, I added hastily, "but I understand all that has been tried, sir."

"Like it here, do you? You don't find it too confining?"

"I like it very much, sir."

He nodded. "Peaceful place. My grandfather brought it over here—you've heard the story. Made a million during the gold rush and brought it over. I grew up here. Great place for birds. Brought up with their songs. Music always meant a lot to me."

So you married a prima donna, I thought, aching with pity, and look what you got!

"I understand Deirdre likes birds when she's having a lucid interval or whatever you call it these days."

"She does some very intelligent bird study, Mr. Mc-Leod."

"She always liked the birds. Even as a little tyke. Cheerful little thing in those days." He looked mournful. "Never see her any more. Hardly see my own son. Hell of a thing for the little chap, having a father just one step away from his grave. I was sixty-one when he was born, Miss Moore, which means I've had my threescore and ten." His eyelids drooped over his eyes, the veins showing blue, and for a moment I thought he slept; but then his eyes winked sharply open.

"Miss Moore. Stay with Deirdre if you can manage it, will you? Martine doesn't care whether the child's alive or dead, and I hate to think of the poor little tyke being shoved around by one hired hand after another. She needs someone young and pretty—ladylike, pleasant. Stay around awhile, will you?"

I said, "I intend to, Mr. McLeod." *And,* I thought, *while I'm around there won't be any more "accidents."*

"I'm an old man, Miss Moore," he said, "and I don't have much reason to think well of women. Stay around awhile. I like thinking that there are still a few decent ones left in the world. Good, plain girls like you, and that nice frumpy little thing we got to look after the boy. Engaged Hester myself, I did." He looked very tired.

I said, "Mr. McLeod, you should sleep now."

"I'll sleep in my grave," he retorted. "Hand me that book there." I gave it to him. It was an ancient, leatherbound copy of *The Confessions of an English Opium Eater,* which seemed a strange choice for a man on the threshold of death. He said, seeing my curious glance at it, "Read this?"

"Not all the way through. I should think something a bit more cheerful, sir . . ."

He laughed, a weak, but pleasant sound. It made me hear the faint echo of Brant's laughter. He said, "You talk

131

like my doctor. Want to put the old man back in the nursery—set him to reading the bloody Bobbsey Twins again! No smoke, no whisky, no good food, not even an exciting book. . . ." His short, exhausted laughter came again. "Well, Miss Moore, at my age you may wish me a short life and a morbid one."

I couldn't help laughing with the old man. He held out his hand.

"Good night, Miss Moore," he said gruffly. "Thank you. Take good care of Deirdre, now."

I promised; and as I crossed the threshold of his room, I found that my eyes were wet.

I had been most thoroughly pulled into rapport with this mad household. I couldn't disentangle myself now if I wanted to; Sanctuary Island had me firmly by the heels, and I was up to my neck in the entangling quicksand of its passions.

Oh, nonsense, I thought; *you've had almost no sleep for two days, and you're a sentimental wreck. Forget it, Susan, and get yourself off to bed.*

Chapter

Twelve

I DON'T KNOW what I expected of Deirdre the next day. I suppose I expected the pattern I had seen before; a tantrum would be followed by sleep and then by forgetfulness. Whatever I had expected, it was soon drowned out in surprise.

The morning after Martine's faint I awoke and dressed, going into Deirdre's room early so that I could be there when she awoke. To my surprise she was awake, lying on her side and looking at the window, down which gray lines of rain were streaming. I made some cheery remark about the weather, which she ignored, turning over to look at me.

"Why did you lock me in my room, Susan?"

So she remembered the whole thing? I said, "Why do you think? So that you wouldn't get out." Damn it, I had had no chance to search her room for the key.

She said, "I've been lying here trying to remember things. Did I dream it, or was Doctor Mason here?"

"He was here," I said.

"Why?"

"We were a little worried about you."

She did not protest, lying with her chin on her hands, thinking. I said, "Do you want to get up? Do you want your breakfast?"

She nodded, flinging one pajamaed leg over the bedside.

"Yes, please. I'm awfully hungry."

"You didn't have much to eat yesterday," I said.

She frowned slightly. "Yes, it seems to be mixed up somehow, as if I'd lost a day someplace. Did I sleep all day yesterday or something?"

"Yes," I admitted.

She looked sharply at me and said, "I'm sick of people never telling me anything, as if I were Jerry's age. I remember people in here yelling, and Doctor Mason, but that's all I remember. About yesterday, that is," she added quickly; "I remember everything else."

"Well, that's fine," I said; "now what do you want for breakfast?"

"I don't care; it doesn't matter," she said impatiently. "Anything." She broke off, then said softly, "I'm sorry, Susan. I don't mean to be cross. I'm just mixed up and trying to remember . . ."

"Don't worry about it, dear."

"And stop saying that," she exploded at me; "I *want* to get it straight in my mind! I've been trying to remember for so long, and then when it starts to get clear, just like the other time, people come and tell me not even to *try* and remember—no, that wasn't you." She frowned again, her brows knotted with the effort. Then she drew a long sigh and walked into the bathroom.

I rang for her breakfast and mine. When it came up, Deirdre was out of the shower and dressed in a crimson sweater and slacks that lent light to the gray rain-lighted room. She stood at the mirror, brushing her hair, then put down the brush and came out to the breakfast table, sitting down and reaching for her cup; then she paused.

"The last thing I really remember clearly, you were giving me hot cocoa and toast," she said. "The cocoa tasted funny. Then what hapened?"

"Then you went to sleep," I said.

"But before that. Let's see. I remember Jerry coming here to supper," she said, pausing with a spoonful of fruit halfway to her lips, "and he said something and I—I—it was like something splitting open inside my head, like a curtain going up—" She broke off, and her face twisted, briefly, painfully, but she mastered it, shook her head, and swallowed the fruit. "I—I don't remember just what happened after that. Until you put me to bed and locked me in my room. I pretended to be asleep so that I could try and remember. Then I got out—"

134

"Since you remember so much, tell me how you got out," I interrupted tartly.

She gave me a surprised stare, then said, "That's right, I never did tell you. It was Margo I told, I guess. I get mixed up sometimes, when *she's* been yelling at me and telling me not to remember things. I'll show you how I got out, if you want me to."

"Eat your breakfast first," I said, not being able to make sense of all this. She took another automatic spoonful of fruit, picked up a piece of bacon and bit into it, then put it down again.

"No. Let me try to remember it all now in the right order, while I can. I knew there was something I'd forgotten, and I thought if I went down there—where it happened—I would remember."

Had she remembered killing Margo?

Hardly daring to move, I watched Deirdre with a frozen fascination. *Let her talk; let her talk. . . .*

"I remembered Margo," she said. "She'd promised me that she'd be back for supper, and she didn't come that night, so I went out to look for her. I—I was afraid to go down the path—you know the place—because I was afraid the tide had come in, and she'd told me never to go down there alone. But I went down. The tide was just starting to come in. . . ."

Her face twisted, and she began to cry, softly, tearlessly. Yet there was none of the incoherent shrieking of terror I had seen before.

"Margo was lying on the rocks," she said. "It was just like the other time. She was all blood, and there were rocks around, and the rocks were all blood. I—" her voice faltered. "I tried to get her to wake up, and then I knew she was dead—"

Oh, God, this again? But Deirdre was serious; her voice was steady, tense, but not maddened.

"I saw someone moving at the top of the cliff, and I hid under the cliff with Margo, I thought they would throw down rocks and—and kill me too, I was frightened, I heard someone coming, and I didn't know who it was. . . ." Her voice trembled, and I thought of the

135

scene Brant had come upon, Deirdre kneeling over the dead girl, clutching a rock covered with blood. . . .

"Only Brant got there first. . . ." Deirdre's voice was just barely a whisper; "and then . . . I don't remember any more."

Mechanically, she picked up her bacon again and ate it, her starved body asserting itself in spite of her nervous inability to concentrate on food. My mind was whirling. The girl told a consistent tale—and it hung together with my own vague suspicions.

Brant had immediately suspected that Deirdre had killed Margo. Yet he had been all too quick to dispose, once and for all time, of the evidence that might have proved the girl innocent of the death of her beloved companion. Martine's words—"Don't be taken in by her"— rang in my mind; but I would back my own knowledge of insane persons and their typical patterns against Martine's judgment. Deirdre was not violent. Always, always, threatened or frightened, she withdrew; she ran away, she shrieked and clung to things and hid under tables, but never, never had she attacked or made so much as a threatening word or gesture.

She had been frightened!

"It was like the other time . . . when I saw him lying there dead. . . ." Something broke in her face, and she began to cry again, helplessly, and suddenly my tentative guess was verified.

Deirdre had seen the murder of that unidentified man . . . the gangster, or whoever he was, the death that Old Jim referred to as "the local horror story." Would a shock like that drive away memory and the power of speech from a sensitive, frightened eight-year-old? Had the child herself been attacked and threatened by the unknown murderers? Had she escaped and hidden, to be found a day and a night later, hiding in the sea caves, reduced by exposure and terror to the level of a scratching, clawing little animal?

I went to her and she clutched at my waist and buried her head against my side, sobbing softly. I patted her, not knowing what to do or say. Finally I said, "It was a long time ago, Deirdre. No one will hurt you now."

"I know." She raised tear-stained eyes. "I realized that, the day you made *her* go away and leave me alone. The day I was playing with Madeline and Amelia. I knew, then, that you wouldn't let *her* in here to hurt me. And it was all right to remember things again."

I listened helplessly, thinking, *This needs a psychiatrist. If the memory block has broken, if Deirdre is not guilty of murder . . . then here is our God-given opportunity to clear up all the shocking mystery of her madness. And of Margo's death. And perhaps even that old murder. A competent psychiatrist, carefully exploring the girl's returning memory . . .*

"I know it was a long time ago," she said. "Margo had cut my hair, and now it's long again. And you've been here—how long have you been here? Sometimes it seems like only a few days; sometimes it seems like a long time."

"A little more than a month," I said. It seemed suddenly like a lifetime to me, too.

"I was talking about last night—or was it the night before? I went down to the sea caves to see if I could find the place and remember. But it's all over now. Why didn't anybody want me to remember?"

I wondered that, too. And a sickening, shocking thought crossed my mind:

Why would Brant jump so quickly to the conclusion that this gentle, frightened child would commit a murder? Or—*was it simply that no one could prove or disprove such a story?*

Had Deirdre been made, then, a scapegoat?

And for whom?

Who *had* killed Margo—and why would Brant try to lay the blame on someone who could never clear herself? It would explain why they did not want Deirdre to get well. It would explain why any signs of returning sanity were greeted without the care they needed. . . .

But Brant? A murderer? After that moment last night, when we had suddenly found ourselves in sympathy, the thought struck cold horror into my bones. I simply could not, would not, believe it.

One thing was certain; this girl must be helped. I

137

calmed her and fed her the rest of her breakfast, meanwhile pondering what to do.

Appeal to Martine was useless. She did not care whether Deirdre were mad or sane, alive or dead. Perhaps once she had cared; and, caring too much, she had had to numb her feelings and grow a mask of indifference. But now she would do nothing to help Deirdre.

I could appeal to Brant—before this, I might have tried. But I had begun to suspect, horribly, that he did not want Deirdre sane, either. He was kind to her—or was that simply a way of keeping close tabs on her memory so that he could tell if it showed signs of returning? And what happened when it showed signs of returning?

Deirdre had somehow—by accident, an accident like Margo's death—got a dose of sleeping pills that could have killed her. And Brant had given them to her! He hadn't even tried to deny it. He had claimed ignorance of their strength—and who could deny that? But knowing Martine as he obviously did, could he really have been ignorant of her possession of strong sleeping pills?

Who, then, could help Deirdre? Dr. Mason? Perhaps, if I told him all I suspected; but then, I might only run the risk of losing my post and being suspected of madness myself! I wondered what I would do, being a hard-headed doctor, if a nurse came to me with any such story as that? I'd probably send the girl packing, as being more lunatic than her patient!

One possibility remained. Last night, old Mr. Alexander McLeod had shown a quite unexpected interest in Deirdre. Would he respond to a plea for proper psychiatric treatment for the girl, help for her returning memory? Could I appeal to him, without the knowledge of either Brant or Martine?

I could certainly try.

Deirdre got up from the table, listening intently, her brow knitted. She walked to the window and looked down at the shore, rubbing circles in the fogged glass and peering through the rain.

"Listen, Susan," she said; "something's going on down there. I hear people running around and yelling, and there are boats—that one is Dr. Mason's boat, and there are a couple of others! Susan, what's happening?"

"I don't know, dear," I said, torn between the desire to go immediately to old Mr. McLeod and my duty to calm my patient and look after her. "Shall I try and find out?"

I left her there, briefly—the telephone was in the hall and I could watch the door, so I had no fear of her getting secretly out of her rooms in case she decided to run away again—and rang through on the house telephone to Mrs. Meadows.

"Is Miss Deirdre better this morning?"

"Much better, thank you," I told her. "Mrs. Meadows, how would I manage to get through to Mr. Alexander McLeod?"

"You'd better ask Mr. Brant about that, Miss."

"I'd rather not bother Mr. Brant with it."

"I'm sure I wouldn't know, Miss Moore," she said stiffly. "Lowden might help you."

"Then may I speak to Lowden?"

"I'll ring him on the house telephone, Miss," she said. But there was no answer, and after a few minutes she said, "He must be busy or with Mr. Alexander, Miss. Perhaps later."

I went back into Deirdre's room, expecting to find her still standing by the window.

She was gone!

I called her name sharply and looked into the bedroom and the bathroom. How had she escaped me again? How had she walked right past me in the hall, to run away again? Had the girl learned to walk through walls? I searched the room, calling her name, calling myself a fool for being taken in enough to listen to her and leave her alone. I suddenly began to feel panic.

"I'm right here," said Deirdre suddenly, behind me. I whirled and saw her standing by the closet door—the closet I had searched just five minutes ago.

Faint with relief—and a growing anger—I demanded, "You little devil, have you been taking lessons from Houdini, or have you learned how to disappear into thin air? Or walk through walls?"

"Oh, walking through walls is easy when you know how," she said nonchalantly, and disappeared into the closet again. I dashed after her, with an incoherent shout, the skin on my forearms rising and prickling. . . .

Deirdre's giggle was high and sweet. "Oh, Susan, Susan! Did I scare you? I'm sorry; it *was* naughty of me. . . . Here, let me show you. I've never dared to use it when anyone else was here, but now that I know you won't tell *her* about it . . ." she moved back into the closet and fumbled at one of the hooks, which was too low for most coats. The hook was placed so inconveniently that I had often wondered why it was there. She twisted it sharply, and the hook slid sideways and the panel moved smoothly aside.

I stood staring, stupefied, at the aperture opening on darkness. Deirdre giggled again.

"I found this when I was little," she said. "What's an old castle without a secret passage or two? Uncle Aleck used to tell me stories about Duncarlie Castle when it was in Scotland. That was just after my mother—" She swallowed spasmodically and broke off, but I noticed and filed away, amazed, that this was the first time since I had known her that Deirdre had referred to Martine other than as "her." Deirdre pulled me through the narrow door.

"Look," she said, and I found myself in a small space, half-lighted by a tiny airshaft. "Look out for the stairs, and here's the other door." She pushed, and I found myself suddenly looking out into my own room. She said, "I came through here and peeked at you the first night you came; only I guess you thought I was a ghost."

"I thought you were a bad dream," I said briefly.

"The stairs lead down, outside the castle," she said; "down into one of the back halls. You can sneak out through a little side door. It's how I got out."

"I thought you had a key," I said. "You scared me out of my wits."

She took my hand confidingly. "I won't do it again. Only please don't lock me in again—it scares me. If you'll tell me you don't want me to go out, I won't do it. I trust you, Susan."

I put my arm around her, suddenly moved. "I trust you,

140

too," I said, not counting that my words might be dangerous. "But sometimes I may have to lock you in. People expect me to. They're afraid you may run away and get yourself hurt."

She pondered this, her small face serious in the darkness
of the secret passage. Finally she said, "All right. If they
think I'm crazy. I know they do. Maybe I was, a little. I
mean—when I get scared and scream at Jerry . . ." her
voice trembled, and she suddenly clung to me. "Did I scare
Jerry?"

"I'm afraid you did," I said truthfully. I was thinking, *If
this girl is crazy, I should be crazy like that.*

"And they probobly won't let me see him again," Deirdre said. "I guess I'll just have to behave myself until they
can trust me again. I'll try, but—I get scared and do
things and say things . . ." She was shaking again, and I
was afraid to pursue this further.

I said firmly, "If you're going to do that, start now by
not crying . . . and by staying in your room when I ask
you to, instead of getting out and running away and scaring us half to death."

"Oh, I won't do that again," Deirdre said; "I think I
found out what I wanted to know." She pushed the sliding
panel shut again; we stood in her closet. "I remembered
almost everything. Next time maybe I'll remember the
rest."

I felt it would be better for her not to talk about it any
more. Saying I wanted another cup of coffee, I poured myself one.

Deirdre, searching in her shelves, brought out her small
bisque dolls again and busied herself looking through their
elaborate costumes. "Susan," she asked suddenly, "how
old am I?"

"I think you're sixteen," I said.

"Is that too old to play with dolls?"

"It depends," I temporized; "in Japan, grown women
make beautiful collections of dolls."

She was fingering the crimson velvet robe of one of the
dolls. She began to dress the brown-haired doll, the one
she called Madeline, in it. She said, "Mother had her picture painted in this one; didn't she?"

141

"She did indeed," I said, surprised; "it's down in the library."

"I forget what opera it's from. I heard it once. She wore a black patch on her eye. I used to have some records of operas, but Margo took them away because I cried when I heard them." She held up a gypsy costume. "This was from *Mignon*," she said. "I remember that because when I was about six, Mother used to play it on the piano and sing it to me. It was when Jerry was a baby. See, I can remember almost everything." She began to sing, in a clear little untrained voice, *"Connais-tu le pays, où fleurit l'oranger . . ."*

I said, amazed, "I didn't know you knew any French. Is that from an opera?"

She said, "I *am* French. Mother is French, and my name is Deirdre Adrienne Clereau. Yes, it's from an opera. . . ." She frowned. "I don't remember all the words; it's something about a land where the lemon trees are in flower. It's about a gypsy girl who was stolen away from her home when she was a baby. I used to love the melody." She went on humming the familiar melody, her eyes slowly filling with tears. "It makes me think of something. . . ."

"It's very sad," I said, inadequately. I did not want to interrupt this flood of reminiscences, but I did not want it to turn into a flood of tears.

Deirdre wiped her eyes, turning over the dresses. "Most of these are just doll clothes," she said. "Janet made them for me. She was a girl who used to take care of Jerry and me. But Mother made up the opera costumes from scraps of the material they were cut from—she used to ask her costumer for them. She used to do a lot of things like that." She was silent, laying the gypsy costume back in the biscuit tin, smoothing the velvet robe on the other doll. "I keep remembering lots of little things. Before I came to the Island . . ." she fell silent and sat staring at her lap, nursing the doll on her knee and humming a scrap of the melancholy little French song again.

In the hallway there were distant sounds of people moving around, and from outside I could hear noises and even distant conversation muffled by the stone. A motorboat started, stopped, started again, and whirred away from the shore. Deirdre said irritably, "I wish I knew what's going on."

"I can try to find out—if you'll promise me not to try to run away again."

"Cross my heart."

I wondered if I were a fool to trust her, remembering Martine's admonition, "don't be taken in by her false little innocent face." I hesitated, and Deirdre said, "Lock me in if you want to. I won't go out the other way." Suddenly she giggled; "It wouldn't do much good, now that you know about it, would it?"

That made sense; I turned back, saying suddenly, "Why *did* you tell me?"

She said very sweetly, "Because I know you won't let anyone in here to hurt me."

I went, turning the key in the lock to salve my own conscience. *Was* the girl mad, with delusions of persecution?

Or were they delusions? Someone apparently wouldn't *mind* if she were dead. . . .

The lower hall appeared to be in commotion, with servants hurrying back and forth; I stood on the stairs, watching, appalled. Dr. Mason came down the other stairs and went into the library; Brant appeared in the door, not seeing me, and at his side was a sturdy, bewhiskered man, his hair gray as iron, briefcase in hand; his dark city clothing was incongruous on the island. He said, "Step in here, Counselor," and the library door closed again. Mrs. Meadows hurried across the hall. I stood baffled on the stairs. Below me, someone spoke my name, and I saw Ross Hunter looking up at me.

"What's the matter, Susan?"

He too was wearing city clothes, and I blinked; they seemed incongruous on the man I knew only in jeans and khaki work clothes. In a white shirt and tie, his blond hair catching the light from the hall chandelier, he looked almost unbelievably handsome. I said, "I think I should be the one to ask what's the matter. What on earth is going on down here? A reunion?"

He laughed, then looked grave. He said, "You didn't know?"

"I've been with Deirdre all night and all morning."

143

"It's old Mr. Alexander," Ross said; "he had a bad attack, and they called Mason and a couple of specialists. They wanted to move him to a hospital on the mainland, but I gather he wouldn't go. That's the family lawyer; so it seems as if it's fairly serious this time. In case you wonder why I'm here, I came to try and see the old man for a few minutes. Orders from up higher—I'm supposed to ask McLeod if he will sell the rest of the island to the bird sanctuary. . . ."

I suddenly remembered Old Jim's words, the first day I had come to the Island: "All them harpies, just waiting around for the poor old gentleman to die . . ." I exploded suddenly, "Can't you let the poor old man die in peace? After he's gone, heaven knows you can do what you like with Martine!"

His face suddenly darkened and grew ugly. He seized my shoulders, drew me to him, and stood staring fiercely down into my eyes. Then he bent and kissed me, hard. I was too amazed to protest.

"That's what I think of Martine," he said, and his voice was rough and furious. "And the hell with Brant, too!"

He let me go, so roughly that I almost fell, and spun away from me on his heel. The study door closed behind him, and suddenly, at the head of the stairs, I saw Martine McLeod standing, looking down at me in tight-lipped rage. Had she heard Ross's words?

But all she said was, "Whatever you want, Miss Moore, it will have to wait until later. My husband is ill, and the household is extremely upset. Please go back and attend to my daughter, and try to keep this pandemonium from upsetting her. We've had enough trouble in the last three or four days, and if she runs away again or has another tantrum, the shock might be a fatal one. So will you please go up and attend to your own business, and do your alley-catting on your own time?"

I said nothing, swallowing the insult without answer. What good would it do to snap back at her? But panic struck through me. If old Mr. Alexander died, where was my hope of appealing to him on Deirdre's behalf? Considering what Martine thought of me, if he should die, my days would be numbered—I meant, of course, my days at

Sanctuary Island would be numbered; what was the matter with me today? And what would happen to Deirdre when I was gone?

Considering the state of the old man's heart, *would it be hard to give him a fatal shock?* Menace seemed to live in every corner of the castle; my heart suddenly began beating hard, and I sped upstairs to Deirdre. Once before she had been given sleeping pills while I literally slept on the job. Dared I leave her alone even for a moment? I literally gasped with relief when I opened the door and found her playing calmly with the small dolls, laying out the doll dresses and costumes, assembling the small skirts and petticoats and trains and cloaks. She looked innocent and happy —too innocent, I thought despairingly, to be a pawn in this dark game. A sick, frightened girl, frightened into madness . . . . And why? What desperate moves were they concealing?

Deirdre looked up in surprise as I switched on the light, trying to banish the grayness from the room. I tried to speak calmly. "It's dark in here," I said; "you'll hurt your eyes if you try to sew."

"What's all the racket about?"

"Nothing much," I said, trying desperately to calm myself again. After all, this was neither the first nor the last time an elderly millionaire with a failing heart had been surrounded by relatives keeping a deathwatch on his last breaths. He must have amazing resilience; he might fool and cheat them all again. "Mr. Alexander McLeod is ill, and your brother has called in a specialist; that's all. May I see that crimson velvet thing?"

The morning dragged on. Carla brought lunch as usual, but she seemed quieter and had less to say than her normal flow of chatter, and I noticed that she looked strangely at Deirdre. The distant voices came and went. Late in the afternoon I heard a motorboat again, and, looking from the window, saw Hester, in her plain English-nanny cape and dress, shepherding little Jeremy, with a packed suitcase, aboard Old Jim's boat. I thought, *At least they have sense enough to send the child away from what might very well be his own father's deathbed.* I did not mention what I had seen to Deirdre. She had troubles enough . . . but at least if she asked for Jeremy I could tell her truthfully that he had been sent to the mainland, that they were not simply keeping him away from her.

Deirdre and I were having an early tea, with some small spice cakes which Mrs. Meadows had brought up (I gathered, from this, that I had been forgiven for Deirdre's escapade), when a knock came at the door. The day had become so tense that I actually jumped.

"Let me answer it, Susan," Deirdre said, jumping up and running toward the door. "Oh—Brant!"

He gave her the usual kiss, but I could see that it was perfunctory and preoccupied. "Let me talk to Susan, there's a good girl? What's that—tea?"

"Would you like a cup?" I asked.

"God, yes. I haven't eaten all day, between doctors and lawyers and what all," he said. He drank thirstily, a handful of cakes in his hand, cramming them down absentmindedly, and took another cup of tea when I poured it.

I asked "How is—?" and broke off, not wanting to speak too plainly in front of Deirdre.

"Not good," Brant said. "It can't be long now. Listen, Susan—two things, and with the chaos around here, nobody's likely to be warning you. First of all, there's a hurricane coming up the coast, which means rain, hail, and unholy weather; so even if we have a calm spell, don't take Deedee in swimming until it's all clear again. It may blow out to sea and miss us; if it hits Sanctuary Island full strength, however, we'll be in for some fun. Not that there's any real danger, of course; Duncarlie Castle has stood up to hurricanes before this. But there might be smashed windows and a lot of noise, and it might scare you—or the kid." He glanced at Deirdre with what seemed honest affection, and I felt bewildered again. "Am I eating up all your cookies, honeybunch?"

"No, go ahead," she said; "I've got all I want."

He took another handful of the cakes, wolfing them down as if he were starving. "Thanks. The other thing is —you know we sent Jerry to the mainland, to be out of the way in case—you know?"

I nodded, and he gestured toward the open door into

146

the hallway. "Listen to that," he said. I strained my ears over the roaring sound of the wind around the heights of the castle and heard a faraway cry, an eerie deep whining sound like that of a child in pain—a giant's child.

"Thumbelina," he said. "Hester absolutely refused to take the dog along, and I can't say I blame her—she's a nuisance in a small boat. But she lies in Jeremy's room whining and howling like a lost soul. I know it's a lot to ask, but for some reason Deirdre seems to be fond of the animal, too. Could you bring her down here? The racket she's making is driving everybody nuts, and I'm a little afraid that if she gets too badly on Martine's nerves right now, Jeremy might come back and, shall we say, find himself minus a dog as well as—"

I nodded, quickly. I didn't know the relationship between little Jeremy and his father—how could a boy of nine regard an old man in his seventies as most children thought of their fathers? But a father's death would be enough shock for one time, and to lose his cherished Thumbelina at the same time would be more than the child could take. "Of course," I said quickly; "Thumbie likes me. Maybe we can keep her quiet. You wouldn't mind having Thumbelina for an overnight guest, would you, Deirdre?"

"Of course not!" she replied. "We'll go get her right away. "Is Uncle Aleck very sick, Brant?"

"I wasn't going to tell you," he said. "Yes, I'm afraid so, Deedee. That's why I haven't had time to spend with you."

"Of course you have to stay with him and mother," she said, and he looked at her strangely, and then at me, as Deirdre moved around the room, saying to herself, "Thumbelina can sleep here, we'll bring down her bed and one of Jerry's coats so she'll feel at home . . . smelling them, you know."

He said, "She doesn't seem to have gone down the way she usually does after a tantrum."

"No, she doesn't," I said, cautiously. Did I dare mention to Brant her rapidly returning memory? I felt acute conflict. This man whom I had thought so rude and arrogant, but who was now looking down at me with lines of fatigue in his face, a cookie still in his hand, which he chewed as he

147

spoke—*could* he be guilty of any such desperate plot as I, in my paranoid fears, had attributed to him?

He said rapidly, "Susan, you're a brick. I haven't even had a chance to thank you for getting me off the hook the other night, when Martine pulled her little trick of crawling into my bed. God only knows what she thinks she's playing at, unless she was trying to get me in Father's bad graces. And now . . ." he gestured. "Seeing Deirdre happy—it means more to me than you can imagine, and now you're even willing to take on that monstrous dog of Jerry's. I think you're the kindest woman I've ever known!"

I laughed a little, flustered. "Oh, that's nothing," I said; "I've got a dog of my own. A cocker spaniel."

"Good grief, I wish I'd known. I'd have told you to bring her along. Where is the poor tyke?"

"Boarding kennel."

"Well, for Heaven's sake, send for her! What's a dog more or less in a place this size? And Deirdre would probably enjoy having her around." I realized that he, at least, seemed to take it for granted that I was a permanency at Sanctuary Island. He went on, saying, "Most women like cats. Wretched, snooty things, I always thought they were. But dogs, now—that's different."

"I've always thought dogs had more personality," I admitted. "Not that I have anything against cats. Except that they always give me an inferiority complex."

He chuckled. "I know just what you mean. One look at a Siamese cat, and I begin to wonder if humans *are* the dominant race, after all." The laughter lighted the lines of strain in his face. I moved to the door, hearing Thumbelina's hysterical howl swelling again, and said, "Come on, Deirdre, let's go and get the poor thing and make her feel loved and wanted."

Deirdre glinted her pixie smile at me. "Yes; before she has a nervous breakdown. One to a family is enough!" she said, and I saw Brant stare after her, wide-eyed, as she set off down the corridor to Jeremy's room. I paused a moment, then hurried after her, just to be on the safe side.

Thumbelina was lying on Jeremy's bed, howling dismally, but when Deirdre bent over the enormous dog and hugged her, the howls subsided into whimpers, and after a

148

little while she began wagging her tail and licking Deirdre's face and hands with her huge, lolloping tongue. Deirdre led the dog along while I struggled after, carrying Thumbie's bed, which was a huge basket that would have held a week's wash for the Dionne quintuplets, and dragging along half a dozen other odds and ends which Deirdre assured me were necessary for the dog's health and well-being.

I blessed the dog's arrival, for the rest of the gray, rainy afternoon passed quickly while Deirdre was soothing, brushing, and grooming the shaggy beast and romping with her. She lay at Deirdre's feet while we ate supper, and I noticed that some lamb-chop bones found their way, surreptitiously, to Thumbelina's cooperative jaws. I said nothing. The rug, thank goodness, wasn't my responsibility, and I was glad for anything that kept Deirdre from brooding too much over her still-unassimilated memories. And when I put Deirdre to bed, Thumbelina insisted on hauling herself up to lie across the girl's feet. I dragged her down at least four times, but she galumphed up again, and finally Deirdre giggled and said, "Let her stay if she wants to. It's a big bed."

"All right." I tucked the blanket around Deirdre. At least, I could count on one thing—if Deirdre suddenly decided on any nocturnal expeditions, Thumbelina would rouse the household with her demands to be taken along too! Maybe a dog was what the girl needed after all!

I woke half a dozen times that night, hearing distant noises and the high, roaring sound of wind in the turrets and towers of the castle, the swash of a roused and angry sea, and the slap and slash of rain against my windows. Twice I tiptoed to Deirdre's door, but the girl was sleeping peacefully, her arms around the neck of the huge, shaggy mutt. Finally I fell fast asleep, to be awakened at eight when Carla came to my door.

"Mr. Brant asked me to tell you, Miss. Mr. Alexander died last night, around three. He asks will you be sure and keep Miss Deirdre to her rooms this morning, so she won't be upset by all the coming and going."

I agreed automatically, feeling the shock that even an expected death must bring. I felt no personal grief, of

149

course, but in my one interview with the old man, he had come through to me in an unusually vivid sense, and it seemed almost like the loss of a friend—and a potential ally for Deirdre. I asked Carla, "Did he say whether I should tell Miss Deirdre? Or should I leave that for her brother to do?"

"I'm sure I don't know, Miss Moore," she said, her manner correct, and I decided to say nothing. Doubtless, Brant would want to break it to his stepsister himself. And I discovered that quite against my will, I was hoping he would come; indeed, I was longing to see him again.

Was I falling in love with Brant?

I was almost grateful to the gale-force winds, the gray rainy sky, and the slap of hail; there could be, of course, no question of going out of doors in this weather for bird-watching or swimming. Thumbelina was company, and I produced some back-issue fashion magazines which kept Deirdre busy trying to copy a Dior model for her dolls. I wondered about the birds in the bird sanctuary. What did they do in weather like this? Were their nests strong enough to keep wind and hail, rain and sleet, out of the way? Or did they die in the rain and cold, or were their nests blown away, leaving them houseless?

I found myself humming a song of my own childhood:

> The North wind doth blow,
> And we shall have snow,
> And what will the robin do then, poor thing?
> He'll sit in the barn
> To keep himself warm—

Deirdre chimed in on the last line:

> And hide his head under his wing, poor thing.

She looked up from her sewing: "I was thinking about the birds too. The gulls will be all right. But some of the land birds will freeze or lose their eggs or their nests if the storm gets much worse. Though some of them will be in the thick underbrush, of course. My father used to sing that song," she added irrelevantly, "when I was *very* small. He taught it to me."

Had she spoken of her father before? I dared not ask

150

questions. I said, "I learned it in school," and the dangerous moment passed over.

The day dragged, and half of the next day went by. The next afternoon, to my surprise, Mrs. Meadows came up. "Mr. Brant wants you downstairs, Miss," she said. "I'm to stay with Miss Deirdre."

Startled, I went down and found—to my surprise—the entire family assembled in the library with Dr. Mason and the bewhiskered individual who had been pointed out to me as the family lawyer. Ross was there, too, again looking strange in his dark business clothes, and I wished I had taken the time to change from the cotton dress I had been wearing.

The lawyer turned to me immediately and said, "You are Miss Moore? My name is Walter Brandwell, of Brandwell, Harper and Stone. Will you sit down, please?"

At my look of surprise, Brant said, curtly, hardly glancing at me, "It seems you're mentioned in the will, Susan. In any case you should represent Deirdre here. Please sit down."

The library was dark, the curtains drawn against the gray spit and hiss of rain beyond. The old-fashioned chandelier, despite electric bulbs, cast strange shadows. Over the grand piano Martine's portrait smiled down at us with inhuman beauty. Martine, beautifully dressed in black, even to her sheer silk stockings, seemed poised and perfect; but her hands betrayed her, for she kept clasping and unclasping them, and I thought of Deirdre's bitten nails for some reason—although Martine's long, oval fingernails were perfect and varnished. She was very close to Brant on the leather sofa. Ross was the only person there who seemed at ease; he was leaning back, relaxed as a cat, in an armchair. Old Lowden was there, too, his face furrowed with unmistakable weeping.

Mr. Brandwell hemmed slightly, opening his briefcase. "As you know," he said, "Mr. McLeod changed his will quite recently. He sent for me three days ago, when he had the first intimations of his death. I may as well add that a few of the provisions of this will are curious, and their reasons are obscure to me; but he insisted that his family would understand why he had framed the will in this par-

151

ticular fashion. Frankly, I will welcome any explanations after you have heard it, ladies and gentlemen."

Martine said, "I've been sure that he was growing senile, Mr. Brandwell. Perhaps his mind had simply given way."

"I assure you, Madam," said Brandwell dryly, "that his mind was quite as clear as I have ever known it to be. Doctor Mason will agree with me. Now, if you please . . ."

Martine fell silent, but again she fiddled with her manicured nails. I wondered suddenly why on earth Ross was here. For that matter, why was *I* here?"

Brandwell opened the document, scanned it briefly, then laid it in his lap. He said, "I think, with your permission, I'll skip all the whereases and the legal language and give you the gist of the bequests. Let me see . . . he starts with the usual formulas, 'I, Alexander McLeod, being of sound mind,' et cetera, et cetera. He directs, of course, that his legal debts shall be paid, and the expenses of his funeral—that's usual—and asks that he shall be buried in the family plot on the mainland cemetery. Then, let me see. . . . First, all the servants who have been here for five years or more receive a hundred dollars apiece. To 'my faithful friend Reginald Winterford Lowden' he leaves the sum of five thousand dollars 'in memory of many years of faithful service' and directs that he shall be kept on by the estate as long as he wishes to remain."

Lowden buried his face in his hands and sobbed aloud.

"There are a few bequests to charity, nothing very much —a thousand here, a thousand there. The next important provision: 'To the Metropolitan Opera Association, Incorporated, whose very existence has given me endless enjoyment, as well as the dubious pleasure of a beautiful wife,' he leaves ten thousand dollars. This is liberal, but of course a drop in the bucket compared to what the total comes to."

I watched Martine's face, but it was unreadable.

"Mr. McLeod"—Brandwell turned to Brant—"you receive Duncarlie Castle, as no doubt you expected. 'To my eldest son, Alexander Brant McLeod, I leave my residence, Duncarlie Castle, the parcels of land immediately surrounding the same, amounting to some five acres and

152

herein enumerated'—I'll show them to you later—'and the residue of my estate except as otherwise disposed.' This makes you a very rich man, Mr. McLeod, even after all other bequests have been accounted for. I'll show you the lists of investments later. Now, 'To my wife Martine Clereau McLeod, an income for life amounting to fifteen thousand dollars a year, to cease upon her death but not upon her remarriage.' He adds a curious provision: 'It is my wish that my son Alexander Brant McLeod offer to his stepmother a home at Duncarlie Castle as long as they shall both desire it.'

Was it a look of triumph that Martine flung at Brant? Brant went on staring down at his knees, disregarding her gaze. Brandwell went on:

"Let's see . . . . 'To my younger son, Jeremy Duncan McLeod, being a minor in his tenth year, I leave the properties on the mainland hereinafter enumerated'—that means a couple of farms and some land which may eventually be in demand for building—'and an income of five thousand dollars a year until his majority, to be expended by the estate in his personal care and education, the income to be paid to him personally after his majority until he shall reach the age of thirty, at which time the capital and any remaining accumulated interest shall be placed at his unqualified disposition.' " Brandwell hesitated. "Originally," he said, "the boy was left a trust fund to be administered by you, Mrs. McLeod, and to revert to the estate in the event of his death before the age of twenty-one, the same provision being made for your daughter. When I questioned the reason for the change, Mr. McLeod told me that you were still a young woman, that you might wish to marry again, and that he would prefer not to burden you with the administration of a large and troublesome estate."

"I think that is damnably unfair," Martine said angrily. "The man must have been out of his mind. It's as if he didn't trust me to administer Jeremy's money properly!"

"Oh, certainly not, Madam!" said Brandwell, scandalized. "I'm sure it was only that he wished to save you the trouble of these complicated legal matters. For instance, the provisions for your daughter are tremendously complicated." He pushed up his glasses and read again:

" 'For my stepdaughter, Deirdre Adrienne Clereau, I leave the following properties'—et cetera, et cetera, et cetera—'to be expended by the estate for her personal care and for the hiring annually of a nurse and companion at a salary of six thousand dollars a year, until she reaches the age of twenty-one, whether or not she recovers her health and reason. Should she recover her health and reason and be capable of profiting by education, a similar sum is to be expended for her education at any school or college chosen by the estate, and the remaining capital presented to her upon her marriage or on her thirtieth birthday, whichever is first. Should she remain in her present emotional condition indefinitely, these funds are to constitute a lifelong trust for her care by a personal companion.' " Mr. Brandwell paused and looked over his glasses. "Now here is another very recent change in the will. Originally it provided that in the event of Deirdre's death before the age of twenty-one, the funds provided for her care would be divided equally between her mother and her stepbrothers. Now, however, it reads as follows: 'In the event that my stepdaughter should die before the age of thirty, the funds provided for her care are to be given to the National Audubon Society, as a free gift in her name.' "

"The man was mad!" Martine exploded, and I sat stunned. He was making it completely unprofitable for anyone to desire Deirdre's death. He had hinted that Martine did not care whether Deirdre lived or died . . . but this will seemed to suggest that he considered someone capable of getting Deirdre out of the way!

"There is more, Mrs. McLeod. 'In the event that it becomes necessary to consign my niece to a mental hospital, the funds necessary to pay for her care there shall be provided in equal share from the estate and from the estate of her own mother, and the properties originally designated for her possession shall be held in escrow until her death, at which time they shall be given, as previously provided, to the National Audubon Society."

Good God, I thought, he was actually making it profitable for Martine and Brant to keep Deirdre at liberty! She couldn't even be put into an insane asylum without the sacrifice of a part of their own properties! Brandwell turned his eyes on me. "There is a codicil referring to you, Miss Moore. This codicil originally applied to a certain Margo Fields, who is, I believe, no longer with Miss Deirdre Clereau."

"She's dead," Brant said briefly.

"I'll read it," Brandwell said. " 'To assure that my stepdaughter shall be kept as far as possible under the care of a single and familiar person, I hereby provide that my stepdaughter's present companion, Miss Susan Moore, in addition to the salary provided, shall receive an additional bonus of one thousand dollars yearly for so long as she shall consent to remain with my stepdaughter, and that in the event that Deirdre shall recover her health and reason to the extent that Miss Moore's services be no longer required, she shall receive a lump sum of fifteen thousand dollars.' "

I literally gasped, before seeing that Martine was as red as a turkey-cock. She rose to her feet. "This whole affair is preposterous," she raged, and I saw the prima donna temperament beneath her controlled fury. "I'm sure it's as illegal as it is insulting. I'll get a lawyer and break that will if it's the last thing I do. . . ."

Brandwell coughed apologetically. "I can understand your feelings, Madam, but please be assured by me, it would be very hard to break this will legally, for Mr. Alexander even provided against such a contingency. 'Should anyone mentioned in this will attempt to break it, he may do so by forfeiting his own share; he shall in this case receive one dollar, the remainder of his share in the estate to be given to the Metropolitan Opera Association, Incorporated, with the request that it be used in part to finance a new production of the Puccini opera *Gianni Schicchi*.' I confess I do not understand this, Madam, but he assured me it would be clear to you. I had assumed that, as you were an opera singer, it was a private joke between you."

Martine's face turned redder and redder, until I was sure she would faint. I half rose, fumbling in my pocket for smelling salts, but instead of fainting, she turned on her heel and strode out of the room, slamming the door violently behind her.

155

Brant whistled and said apologetically, "I say, Brand-well, I'm sorry that happened. Martine is high-strung. . . ."

"Oh, please don't apologize, my dear sir; the lady has had a trying day. I'm sure she will realize that actually she has simply been spared a good deal of legal bother and trouble. I am accustomed to families being angry about wills. After all, they come along when the family is under a good deal of strain."

He glanced at Ross, saying, "Are you Mr. Hunter, from the Forestry service? There is a small bequest here to the United States Forestry Service; he has left about eight acres of the Island to the bird sanctuary 'in partial compensation to the United States Government for the legal tax loopholes from which I have profited all these years.' The old gentleman had a sense of humor, I should say, Mr. Hunter."

Ross laughed, not thinking it was funny. His eyes were fixed on the door through which Martine had vanished. I wondered if he had expected Martine to get the majority of the old man's estate. Would Martine now choose Brant instead? Ross's look was almost murderous for a moment; then he said, "Well, that settles that. My sucessor will profit by it, I suppose, not me; I'm leaving the island this summer. I've been here long enough."

"I'm sure it will be a great loss," Brandwell said, form-ally rising to take his leave. "Mr. Brant, I am at your dis-posal whenever you choose to consult with me about the estate."

Ross stood up, too, turning to me. "So you come in for a few plums too," he said, "as long as you stay with the kid, Susan? Fat lot of good it will do you, tucked away here!" He smiled bitterly, adding, "I've decided to get out. By now it should be all right."

"Are you going soon?" I asked. I realized I would be sorry to see him go. He was so marvelously uninvolved with the complicated plots and entanglements of the Mc-Leods; I realized I had come to depend on him for a ref-uge against the overstrained atmosphere of Sanctuary Is-land.

156

"Yes." He dropped his voice so Brant could not hear. "But I want to see you before I go. When can I talk to you alone?"

"I don't know. Deirdre is upset by all this," I said. "I'll call you—"

Brant interrupted, saying, "I knew my father was intending to do that, Ross; that's why I told you before that I couldn't do anything about it."

Ross said, "What in the devil was all that about some opera or other—*Gianni Schicchi?* I never heard of it. Of course I'm no opera fan. . . ."

"Damned if I know," Brant said; "Maybe it *was* some private joke of Father's. As near as I can remember, Gianni Schicchi is a one-act opera by Puccini—you know the chap who wrote *Madama Butterfly* and *La Bohème*—a funny farce about an old man who was surrounded by poor relations crying crocodile tears, and after he was dead, they hired a professional nogoodnik—Gianni Schicchi—to forge a will in their favor. . . . Oh, my God!" he said, breaking off and dropping into a chair.

I thought he was realizing, with shock, the extent of his father's persecution mania—and then, with even more shock, *I* realized that he was almost howling with laughter. "And Gianni Schicchi turns the tables on them by forging a will—in favor of Gianni Schicchi!" He rocked back and forth with laughter. "Oh, my God! If the old man was senile when he wrote *that,* I'm Enrico Caruso! What a ghastly joke! God, what a ghastly joke to make! Dying with a last laugh on all of us, the old dear!" He laughed almost hysterically, tears running down his face, and suddenly he was almost sobbing himself.

"Poor old Father; poor old guy! Oh, my God, Susan . . ." He grabbed me and held on to me, and for a moment I forgot that he was a rude, arrogant man ten years my senior, and held him as I would have held Deirdre. "Did he think *I* wanted his money? Oh, Dad, Dad . . ."

Ross had quietly tiptoed out. I held Brant against me silently, my feelings about this man undergoing another violent upheaval. Was he a cold-blooded murderer—or a man who had panicked at an accident—or was he simply

157

an innocent bystander, loving his family, mourning for his father?

I did not know. I only knew my heart ached for him, and legacy or no, I wished his father were still alive.

For more reasons than one. . . .

Chapter

Thirteen

A DEATH CARRIES a certain momentum with it. Things happen in a certain way and in their own time. Old Alexander McLeod had been a recluse for years—but he had not always been one, and he had friends and neighbors. Some of them came out of genuine courtesy, to pay their last respects to a man they once had known. Others came, I suspected, out of curiosity, to see what the inside of a genuine old-world castle looked like, to say that they had been inside the mystery place of the islands, or just because he had been alive and now he was dead.

I hate funerals. I had hardly known old Mr. McLeod, but I remembered that brief acquaintance with kindness, and I had no desire to see the unholy show that our society puts on over its corpses. I welcomed the good excuse I had, to say that Deirdre was not in any state to attend a family funeral. I kept her out of the way of the comings and goings, and I was glad that either Martine or Brant had had the good taste to keep little Jeremy away from the funeral.

But the funeral isolated us. I had to keep Deirdre in her own rooms much of the time. She was curiously silent, but now and again she would speak of events of the past, and I realized that the fog around her memory was lifting. Slowly, the girl was coming along the path that separated past from present, bringing herself into today. I resolved that when all this was over, I would talk to someone—perhaps old Dr. Mason—frankly and insist that psychiatric treatment be obtained for the girl. She couldn't cure herself, but if the mental block of memory were lifted, could she not come into the normal world?

For the present I could do nothing. I wanted to talk to Brant; with the memory of holding him in my arms that night, I had a curiously physical sense of his presence; I almost ached for him. And yet . . . and yet . . .

At the back of my mind the suspicion lodged and would not be denied. *Had Brant killed Margo and laid the blame on Deirdre?* As often as I told myself he was incapable of such a thing, I remembered that a woman's judgment, when her female chemistry has her attracted to a man, is not reliable. I didn't want to believe it of Brant because I was falling in love with him. It was as simple as that.

Either way I was an accessory to murder—if it had been murder. But was I required to do anything about it, when police court and coroner's jury had pronounced it accident?

If Deirdre recovered her memory . . .

Alexander McLeod was laid in the earth, and I was shocked at how little difference it seemed to make in Dun-carlie Castle. It was as if he had never lived. I wondered what Martine would do now. Fifteen thousand a year— it was a niggardly allowance for a millionaire's wife. And yet, would she want to remain here with a stepson who had pretty obviously rejected her play for him?

Ross called me twice during this difficult time, but both times I had to put him off. He seemed blessedly uninvolved in this business, and I longed to confide in him. But the telephones at Duncarlie Castle were all on the vast network of house phones. How could I be certain that a servant, on some innocent errand, might not pick up the phone and eavesdrop? And could I confide my suspicions of Brant over this open line?

And there was the memory of Martine in his cabin; so in a way it was a relief to be able to say, truthfully, that I couldn't leave Deirdre while the house was in this uproar.

He confronted me on the beach one day when I was swimming with Deirdre; and while the girl romped out of earshot with Thumbelina, Ross demanded, "Why are you avoiding me, Susan?"

"I'm not," I said. "It's only that with things upset like this, I can't leave Deirdre."

His face twisted vitriolically. "They've got you hogtied with that legacy too? You'd tie yourself down for life to a crazy kid for their money? Is everybody around here tied down by that dead man's money?"

I resented that. Stiffly, I said, "It isn't the money, Ross. I'm fond of Deirdre, and I don't like the idea of seeing her shuffled from hand to hand." Then I exploded, "For Heaven's sake, as a licensed and registered nurse I can make twice this much in a year if I want to choose my cases carefully enough! Do you think a paltry seven thousand would keep me here if I didn't want to stay?"

He put his hand on my arm, and the touch was electric. "And suppose I said—I'm leaving; come away with me?"

My mind was suddenly in turmoil. All I could think was a confused, *It's not fair; it's not fair to ask me this now, out in plain sight of the girl and the dog and the house.* All I could think of to say was, "What about Martine?"

His eyes suddenly glinted with a steely look I had never seen in them before. "What the hell—*what* about Martine?"

"I saw her footprints in your cabin. And smelled her perfume."

He drew a long breath, controlling himself. He said, "I never claimed to be an angel. I've been on this damned island for years, and she's—well, she's a young and beautiful woman married to an old and feeble man. I'm only human. If you have as much knowledge of human nature as a nurse should have . . ."

It wasn't that I was a prude. I could see his point. Damn it, I could even see Martine's, though it still seemed a bitch trick to me to sneak around behind the back of the old man who supported her in luxury. But I wasn't the keeper of Martine's morals. I wavered, and he bent close to me, persuasively. "Do you think I care a pin about Martine, aside from the fact that she's been *here,* and I had to stay? Let's clear out, Susan! Leave the whole crazy batch of them! I can show you a world you never dreamed about!"

I could only say weakly, "Ross, I don't know; it's not fair to spring this on me—"

"This is so sudden!" he mocked savagely. "Or is it Brant you're hoping to snag? After all, he's a millionaire. . . ."

I rose angrily. "I don't have to listen—"

He was immediately contrite. "Susan, don't go like this—"

"I have to see to Deirdre," I said, and called to her. As she ran to me he caught my shoulders, bending over me and saying urgently, "Don't say no now. Listen. Come to my cabin. Give me a chance to convince you—"

I promised, wrenching free as Deirdre ran up, the huge dog frisking and lolloping at her heels. I felt shaken, my heart pounding. *Ross*. Was I glamored by him, or was it only that he was outside the mad and haunted life of the castle? Or—an unworthy thought scuttled like a rabbit across my mind—had he been waiting to see if Martine, after the death of her elderly husband, would be worth the having, and decided that a mere fifteen thousand wasn't worth it?

I put it away resolutely, turning to my charge. "Did you have a nice swim?" I asked. "You look like a thundercloud, Deedee."

"I don't like that man," she said sullenly, and that was all I could get out of her, then, or while she collected her beach towel and robe and we went up toward the house. But something was working away behind her closed face. She said, "Is he in love with you, Susan"

"I don't know, dear," I said honestly, and she seized my hand and clung to it. Her possessive jealousy was, I supposed, only to be expected. Sixteen she might be, but with the long gap in her memory she was nearer to eight or ten in emotions. I was really all that Deirdre had.

She said, "Why don't you marry Uncle Brant? Then you'd belong here." I laughed a little, shakily. "He hasn't asked me, darling."

She scowled. "No. I suppose *she* . . ." she fell silent again. We came into the dark corridor of the house, and I saw with dread that Martine was standing in the hallway, her hand on the house telephone.

"Oh, suit yourself, Mrs. Meadows," I heard her say; "if you can't get asparagus, make it something else; what does it matter? What's the point of a housekeeper if I have to settle every little detail myself!" She banged the receiver down, turned and saw us, and her face took on the usual wary, tense look as she looked up at Deirdre.

I watched Deirdre carefully. Was she about to start to scream, to run and hide, to try to crawl beneath a table?

162

To my amazement, she stood her ground, looking past me at her mother.

She said, "You think you'll marry Brant, don't you, Mother?" Her voice was superficially steady, but I detected a note of shrillness, even of fear, in it. I was shocked at her words—and yet, Deirdre actually standing up and defying someone she feared most? Calling her *Mother?* Even if the words were sarcastic, was that not a healthy sign of vanishing fear?

But their effect on Martine was quite different. She went crimson with rage and snarled, "You impertinent little cat, how dare you—"

I said peacefully, "Please, Mrs. McLeod . . ." and turned to Deirdre. "Hush, dear; don't be rude."

"I'll teach her to talk that way," Martine said furiously, advancing on us, and Deirdre stepped backward, her hands going up in automatic, frightened self-protection. I watched in horror; was Martine *trying* to touch off the girl to a fit of shrieking hysteria? I laid a restraining hand on Martine's arm. Deirdre, backed against the wall, her eyes wide and blue in her terrified small face, swallowed and I saw her mouth move.

"Will you kill him, too, Mother? Will you kill me? The way you killed—"

With a scream of inarticulate rage, Martine was on her daughter, her clawed fingers raking at Deirdre's eyes. Then, her hands biting into the girl's shoulders, she shook Deirdre back and forth, back and forth, until the girl's head flopped limply, like a rag doll. Deirdre was sobbing in broken, inarticulate noises, her breath coming in gasps, her eyes showing white all round the pupil. I broke the frozen horror that held me. I had handled violent patients before this. I grabbed Martine under the arms, jerked her back with a wrestling hold, got a hammerlock on her, and dragged her bodily off the cowering, whimpering Deirdre. Martine struggled madly, her face contorted with wrath. "You heard her; you heard her—damn you, let me go! . . ."

Maddened, Martine had almost maniacal strength, and I began to wonder seriously if I could hold her—but help came from an unexpected source. Thumbelina streaked down the hall, belly down, and leaped up on Martine, knocking her to the ground! I shouted at the dog, knocking her away. Deirdre had collapsed in a forlorn, broken little heap on the ground, a limp little pile from which came soft, sobbing whimpers. I was blazing with rage. I hauled Martine roughly to her feet.

"Stay here, Thumbelina!" I ordered the dog peremptorily, and she nosed, whining, at the heap that was Deirdre. I manhandled Martine into the library, kicked the door shut, and shoved her down, hard, into a chair.

She looked up at me, her face congested with rage. "How dare you!" she spat.

"How dare *you!*" I retorted, righteous fury making me careless of what I did or said. "Why, you heartless, sadistic woman! If you've frightened Deirdre into another of her fits, you—good God, Mrs. McLeod, do you call yourself a mother? I—I wouldn't give you a kitten to raise!"

"You heard what she said to me, the false, lying little bitch—"

"I heard it," I blazed, "and you yourself are always telling me to take no notice of what Deirdre says! Yet you fly into a rage at a rude remark from a child you know is mentally ill! So what does that make you? Deirdre may be mad; you are supposed to be a grown woman, and sane! Now you listen to me!" I stood over her, my hands on my hips, literally shaking with wrath. "If you ever lay a hand on that poor child again, I swear before God, I will have you hauled up in front of the Society for the Prevention of Cruelty to Children! Were you *trying* to frighten the girl into a fit?"

"She accused me of murder!"

I said, trying to be calm, "Mrs. McLeod, you yourself have said again and again that Deirdre is subject to delusions. She is getting better; her memory is coming back. But you cannot expect that it will happen all at once. If you could show her patience and love, instead of trying to see if you can outdo her in irrational accusations and wild talk, she *might* get better."

"How long do you think you will be lording it around here?" she spat at me. "Or have you managed to get Brant on your side against me? I notice how cleverly you wormed your way into my husband's—"

"Mrs. McLeod, for Heaven's sake!" I looked at her with undisguised disgust. "I think you are hysterical. A very little more of this, and I shall begin to wonder whether you aren't as subject to delusions as Deirdre is! What sort of a nurse would I be if I failed to protect my patient from physical violence—and from her own mother, at that? One would think you were *trying* to frighten the girl into a fit, that you were afraid she would recover her memory! In Heaven's name, what are you afraid she will say?" I stopped myself, realizing that I was almost as wound up as Martine. I turned my back on her. "I must get back to Deirdre. But remember what I say. If you ever again lay a hand—a *finger*—on your daughter, you'll find yourself explaining it in Children's Welfare Court!"

I slammed the library door behind me and ran down the hall toward Deirdre, who was still lying on the floor, sobbing hysterically. Thumbelina was whining and nosing anxiously at her, licking her white face with an anxious pink tongue. I picked Deirdre up bodily in my arms, and she shook with gasping sobs. I carried her up the stairs. She was pitifully light in my arms. I laid her down in her own bed, and, because I knew Thumbelina would rouse the whole castle if I barred her, let her come too. After a while, Deirdre's eyes opened weakly and she patted, absently, at the dog's big muzzle.

"Susan," she said between gasps, "now you can see. It was like the other time. She hates me, she hates me . . . she shook me and shook me until I couldn't even talk, I couldn't think straight. . . . She used to come to me when no one knew, she used to pinch me and shake me and tell me not to say a word, tell me I couldn't remember anything. . . ."

"Hush, darling. Hush. Don't think about it." What could I say? Martine did hate Deirdre; I could see that. But these wild accusations—how could I blame Deirdre for delusions about her mother, if the woman would treat a demented child in such a way? And it was not the first time. I could see that now. Deirdre was frightened almost to death. Had Martine, before she new the seriousness of Deirdre's condition, ill-treated her this way?

"Don't tell me it never happened!" Deirdre moaned.

"Darling. Deirdre, listen. I fixed her; she'll never dare lay a hand on you again," I reassured her. "I promise you, she won't ever dare to touch you. I fixed it so she'll never dare."

The room was dark with the gloom of rain outside, a dark, overcast sky, and heavy clouds; I drew the curtains and switched on the lights. Then I saw with horror that there was actually blood on Deirdre's face, deep scratches from Martine's long nails. Shocked beyond words, I silently sponged the wounds and painted them with iodine.

No slum mother on welfare would attack a sick child like this, I thought in furious disgust. *Martine must be as disturbed as Deirdre—and I'd like to see that someone finds out about it!*

Deirdre's sobs had subsided; she flinched slightly as I put the stinging antiseptic on the scratches, but that was all. But she clung to my hand, almost frantically. "She won't get me again, will she? You won't let her?"

"No, dear."

"How can you stop her?" She wet her pale lips with a small pink tongue. "She's my mother. . . ."

"Listen," I said firmly; "mother or no mother, if she tries to hurt you again, she'll find out, Deirdre, that there are laws to protect—you know that you've been sick, you sometimes imagine things—"

Her hands flew to the scratches, and her eyes were reproachful, shocked. "I didn't imagine *this!* . . ."

"No, no," I said quickly. "I mean; there are laws to protect—sick people. And little girls. I'm a registered nurse, you know, dear, and I've been put in charge of you." I wondered briefly if it were a breach of ethics to discuss my employer with my patient, then decided that Deirdre should know that she was protected, legally if necessary. The girl's sanity was evidently returning, and above all, her peace of mind must be protected.

"You see, Deirdre, when people are sick, as you've been, they're usually sent to hospitals; and the doctors and nurses there have the right, by law, to do what's best for them, no matter what their family might say or do. I'm a nurse, and I've been put in charge of you; and all I would have to do is to tell any court how your mother had attacked and frightened you, and the judge would make out an order saying that she was to let you alone—that she couldn't even come near you unless she promised to behave herself the way a mother ought to behave around a sick girl. Do you understand that?"

"And—you'd do that for me?"

"If she ever lays so much as a finger on you again, I most certainly will. And I told her so."

Deirdre drew a long sigh of relief and lay looking up at me. "I've been so afraid of her," she said, swallowing hard. "It was just like the other time. She shook me and shook me until I couldn't even talk. . . ."

Her face twisted, and she began to sob violently, tearing sobs that seemed to shake her whole body to pieces. She put up her hands protectively as if to ward away some violent attack. She screamed suddenly, "No! No! No, Mommy, Mommy, don't, don't—Papa! Papa!"

Shocked and terrified at the suddenness of this attack, I caught the screaming, shrieking child in my arms and held her tight.

"No, no, darling—you dreamed it," I soothed; "no one is here. No one is hurting you—"

Her eyes rolled back, staring at someone I could not see. "No, no . . . oh, his head is all bloody, his head— what are you doing? Mommy! Mommy!" She shrieked, a terrible scream that seemed to rip her throat out, cowering and sobbing. Wordlessly, I held her tight. Then, with a gasp and a shudder, the eyes suddenly blinked, and Deirdre was lying back in my arms. She was white to the lips and shaking, but her eyes were level and sane.

In a shaking voice, she said, "No, that was years ago; years ago, it must have been. . . . Susan, she killed him! *She killed him!*"

Aghast, horrified at the drama reenacted before my eyes, I could only whisper, "Who?"

"My father! Oh, Papa! Papa!" She was sobbing again, not the horrified, mad sobbing, but a strange, almost noiseless crying I had never seen before. "When she shook me

167

it was so much like the other time—I hit my head on the rocks, I think—she kept telling me not to talk, not to say a word, not to say a word. . . . And he was lying there with his face all bloody. . . ."

"Deirdre, do you know what you are saying?" I demanded, knowing that I had gone as white as the child.

"You don't believe me either," she said; "you think I'm crazy, everybody thought I was crazy. . . ." She swallowed hard, clenching her small fists, trying desperately to compose herself. "Susan, listen; it's what I tried to show Margo, and then she went back there to see, and—and I found her dead like the other time, and I was so frightened I couldn't tell anybody, and I—I think I must have been crazy for a while. But you're not afraid of—of mother, and I can show you . . ."

Oh, God, I thought, what new madness has Martine touched off now? If I only dared go to Brant . . .

"Deirdre," I said, "you've been sick. I think you have bad dreams and you imagine—"

Her voice held the bleakness of despair. "I told you you wouldn't believe me either. But I can show you. I can tell you—"

It flashed through my mind; whatever this child had seen seven years ago at the time of the murder, it might provide the clue to her madness and her lack of memory. Or was this a preliminary to a repetition of the tragedy of Margo Fields? Against my will I wondered, *Will she suddenly attack me, too?* But I was not afraid. Margo had presumably not been warned. If Deirdre turned on me, I could handle her . . . and if she could give me some clue, it might prove the key to her returning memory, her returning sanity.

"Tell me," I said.

She said, "I—I spoke of Papa. When I was five, Mother left him. She was a singer then, and one day he—he just went away, but he told me that some day he would come back to me. Then Mother married Uncle Aleck, and we came here to live." She looked at me shrewdly and said, "Uncle Aleck is dead now, isn't he?"

"Yes. We didn't tell you. We were afraid of upsetting you."

"We came here to live. Then one day I got a letter from Papa. It said that he was coming here to see Mother . . ." her face suddenly twisted, "and to take me—away to live—with him. . . ."

"Deirdre—"

"I saw where Mother buried the box with the letters!" she flung at me; "I can show you! I can prove it to you! I talked with him there in the sea caves! . . ."

She leaped up from the bed suddenly. "Come with me! I can show you! I can find the box. . . ."

"Deirdre, it's raining; it's cold—"

"You don't believe me," she accused; "you don't *want* me to find it!" She paced the floor in agitation, turning on me angrily. "I've got to, Susan! If—if I dreamed it or imagined it, I want to *know!* I—I've been lying awake nights trying to remember, wondering if I dreamed it, if I'm really crazy the way they say!" She came and caught my arms, pleadingly. "Oh, Susan, please, please, help me find out, let me prove to myself whether I really remember it or whether it was just a—a crazy nightmare. . . . Oh, I *want* it to be a nightmare, but when she shook me, I saw it all again. . . ."

Against my better judgment, I said slowly, "where do you want to go, Deirdre?"

"To the sea caves. Where I found Margo dead, where *she* buried the box—where *she* killed him while I hid in the cave watching her smash his head in with a rock!"

"Your father?" Against my will, the gripping conviction in her voice swept me along.

"My father! *She* killed him, she killed him there, and I watched from the sea caves and hid in the rocks. . . . And then she found me and she knew I saw her!" Deirdre, white and shaking, pulled at me. "Susan, Susan, take me there so I can remember if it happened or if it was only a bad dream, or I'll never know again whether anything is real!"

169

Chapter

Fourteen

I STARED AT Deirdre in horror, wondering if a nurse had ever been faced with such a problem. If I humored her, was I not falling into a delusion too? And yet—and yet . . .

Deirdre wanted to test the reality of her own beliefs. That could be a sign of returning sanity; when she found nothing there, it might dispel the illusion once and for all.

And—the very thought sent ice water trickling down my spine—if the child was telling the truth, if she had actually seen what she said, and now she remembered, what would Martine do now that the story was out?

Might she not actually murder Deirdre herself? I had seen Martine turn into a raving madwoman at Deirdre's accusation. *Why?*

It was worth testing. The worst that could happen would be Deirdre's refusal to believe that there was nothing there—and at least I would know then, for certain, that I *was* dealing with a child actually maddened, and not, as I was beginning to suspect, merely driven mad with terror.

I said, keeping my voice steady, "All right. Get your coat. It's cold. Whatever you want to show me, I'll look at it."

As she opened her coat closet, Thumbelina started frisking around. Deirdre looked at her, smiling shakily. "She thinks she's going for a walk too!"

I said firmly, "No, Thumbie; not this time." I went to my room for my own coat and, making a sudden decision, charged a hypodermic needle from my kit with a strong sedative. If Deirdre, her delusion attacked, should go into another fit of raving, I wanted to be sure I could handle her. That was why I had left Thumbie behind—having seen the dog fly at Martine when she touched Deirdre, I wasn't anxious to cope with an angry Newfoundland if I found myself having to restrain the girl physically.

The rain was cold, and the endless birdsong on the island was silenced to a few desolate chirps. I remembered the hurricane warnings. Was this the edge of the oncoming storm, or had it blown out harmlessly to sea, leaving us merely the fringe storms? Deirdre walked silently, her hands thrust into the pockets of her white raincoat, across the beach and up the path to the crest of the hill that led down to the sea caves. Here she faltered, turning to me, her steps slowing.

"Susan—I'm afraid. . . ."

I said, "You don't have to go down there. We can go back to the house."

She looked at me as if I had struck her, but she said only, "No. I—I have to. Only—hold my hand, will you?"

Silently I stretched my hand to her and felt her clasp my fingers with her small, ice-cold ones. I had seen patients like this, going to the shock treatments they feared. She moved slowly, step by jerky step, as if dragging her feet through a weight of molasses; but she kept moving. Her face was white and set, and her eyes seemed sunken and bruised. Her hair, lank elflocks in the damp sea wind, straggled against her cheek, and I wondered if I were letting myself be led on a wild-goose chase by a lunatic, if it would end in a very ugly struggle with a very sick girl. Step by slow step, Deirdre clinging to my hand almost desperately, we moved down the path to the strip of beach.

The tide, I noted almost automatically, was low, but I was not sure whether it was going in or out. I tried to remember what it would be at this time of day, but my attention was on Deirdre, who had suddenly dropped my hand and begun to run toward the largest of the sea caves. I uttered a mental self-imprecation and fled after her, but she stopped at the entrance and stood staring around as if to orient herself.

"Here was where Papa came," she said under her breath, "and I stood here and talked to him. We found some shells. They should be in the upper cave."

"Wouldn't the sea have washed them away, Deirdre?"

171

She pointed. At the back of the cave was a high slope, with what looked like rough rock steps leading upward. She said, "If you climb that—it isn't easy—you get into an upper cave. The sea can't come up there. . . ." She started to scramble up the rocks. I followed, watching her long bare legs disappear through the jagged hole in the ceiling of the cave; I followed, hesitating, on my guard lest she suddenly attack me as I emerged through the opening. . . .

The upper cave was large, rocky, and well lighted from an opening in the cliff high above. Our voices echoed as if in the chancel of a great church, as Deirdre whispered, "Look—on that shelf. Here are the shells. . . ."

I followed her glance, and in the dimness I saw, on the rock ledge, an assortment of small pink shells laid out in the form of a five-pointed star. She picked up one of them and pointed, in silence. On the back, with some sharp instrument, an adult hand—the lettering was too small and delicate for any child or for Deirdre's own sprawl—had incised D.A.C. 1958.

"See?" she said in a whisper; "my initials, where Papa made them that day."

I felt a *frisson* of horror run down my spine. *Deirdre Adrienne Clereau. 1958*—seven years ago.

The year of the murder.

And had no one been in the upper sea cave since?

She drew a sigh of relief, and in the dim light from the hole in the cliff, her face relaxed. She said in a whisper, "I didn't dream *that*, anyhow."

She knelt and suddenly began scrabbling in the sand. I stared, watching her, saying in amazement, "You'll break your fingernails—"

"Give me a stick, then," she said logically. "Look." She pointed to the mark on the wall. "I marked the place, before *she* came back. . . ."

There was a crude *X* on the wall—marked with the white chalky stuff of shell, I supposed. The sandy layer silted up in the corner of the cave had not been disturbed in—how long? Deirdre scrabbled on, and finally she gave a cry of triumph.

"It's here! Susan, it's here!" she gasped. "I didn't dream it; it's here. . . ."

And then her face collapsed and she began to sob softly. *"Then she did kill him. . . ."*

Paralyzed with horror, I bent over what looked like a rusted metal deed box. The lock, long rusted in the salt sand, came apart in my hand, and some papers, damp but legible, fell out on the sand. I reached for them.

The top one was a long envelope bearing the return address of the National Audubon Society in Philadelphia. It was addressed to Deirdre Clereau, and I drew it out hesitantly, looking at Deirdre. The letter was typewritten; I moved over beneath the opening in the cliff wall, so that I could read the words. Glancing out, I saw that the strip of beach had narrowed; the tide was coming in.

I read:

> Dearest Deedee,
>
> Did you know that I had found out where you were? A bird sanctuary is a good place for my little bird, but your mother had no right to take you there without telling me. I am coming to talk it over with her, and with you. Don't tell your mother about this letter; I have written to her before, and she has refused to answer me. Meet me on the side of the island by the sea caves tomorrow afternoon; if I'm not there by the time the tide comes in, come the next day.
>
> With all my love,
>
> Papa.

A wild surmise was coming over me. I looked quickly at the other letter, which was addressed to Martine. I had no further compunctions; so I opened it and read:

> My dear Martine:
>
> It has not been easy for me to trace you, and no doubt you will be angry that I have finally succeeded. Rest easy; I have no desire for a scandal— no more than I had when you left me, taking your daughter, for no reason at all. I had never interfered

173

with your career; I only wished to assure that Deirdre would be given proper care.

Bigamy is a serious charge. I have made inquiries, so please don't try to put me off with claims of a Reno or Mexican divorce; you had not even the right to presume my death until seven years had passed without hearing from me. I wonder if you ever even bothered to mention my existence to Alexander Mc-Leod? I have too little knowledge of millionaires to know whether he would consider a little thing like a previous undivorced husband an obstacle in his way.

You wanted riches and luxury; you have them. I am not blackmailing you; I will go quietly away and get the divorce you failed to get. However, I insist upon one thing. I must be allowed to see Deirdre whenever I wish, and she must be allowed to visit me. If you make any of your famous scenes, or if you think you can keep the whole thing more secret by refusing to acknowledge that I still exist, then Alexander McLeod will find out, from me or from my lawyers, that he has married a woman who is at least a bigamist and that your son by him is illegitimate.

I have no more interest in you. But I will see you in hell before I let you keep my daughter in ignorance of whether I am alive or dead.

If you refuse to answer this letter as you have refused to answer others, you must take the consequences.

Yours respectfully—I don't think—

André Clereau.

The letter fell from my fingers. I could imagine the effect of such a letter on the proud Martine—and I could imagine the face of old Alexander McLeod when he was told that his prima-donna prize, the wife he had worn like a jewel in his castle, was a common bigamist. I looked briefly at the other papers. Letters, a letter from a legal firm briefly informing "Mrs. Clereau" that it was urgent that she communicate with her husband with respect to the custody of their daughter, and a photostatic copy of

174

Deirdre's birth certificate, giving her year of birth as 1947 —which made her two years older than I had believed. Perhaps Martine had not liked to be thought as old as that?

Had Martine buried these here? Why had she not returned to burn them? Or had she, like Deidre, conceived a horror of the scene of the crime? I looked at Deirdre. She was standing, fixed and white, staring.

"I came here," she whispered, "and Papa and I found the shells. He told me Mother was not really married to Uncle Aleck, because it was against the law to marry another man while he was alive, but so that there wouldn't be any scandal, he was going to get a divorce. He said it was against his religion, but he didn't want to—to make Jerry into a bastard, publicly. Only he said I would be able to come and see him, whenever I wanted to. He wanted to know all about the bird sanctuary, and he said he would come here and look it all over with me some day."

She trembled, and her cold hands sought for mine. "The tide was coming in. I told Papa we had to leave before the tide came too far up, and we went down into the lower cave. Then I heard Mother calling me. I—I was afraid she'd spank me; so I—Papa said not to be scared, he'd talk to her, and he went out to the edge of the cave and called to her—'*Maritine!*' like that. She—she turned white, and they started talking very fast in French. I—I was too far away to hear, but I heard her say *vous* instead of *tu*, so I knew she was awfully angry. Then all of a sudden she *screamed* at him: . . ."

Deirdre's face contorted and she gasped out, in a voice curiously like Martine's: "*Fils d'enfer! C'naille! Cochon! Je vous v'rrai la tête au cul de diable avant que j'vous laisse m'tromper. . . . Dieu me damne,* he thinks I'm a widow and by God I'll make myself one first. . . ."

Deirdre began to tremble; I held her tightly. She gasped, "She picked up a rock. . . . He thought she was fooling, he laughed at her and said, 'How you show your fishwife origins! Or are you rehearsing a new opera?' And then she—she smashed the rock down—oh, Susan, he was still laughing at her, he was still laughing . . . and she smashed his head in, she went on hitting him and hitting him and hitting him. . . ."

I caught the girl in my arms, holding her head to my breast, rocking her back and forth while she sobbed, helplessly. I was cold with horror, but I could no longer doubt. How could a child of eleven invent such a tale? How would a child of that age invent low patois French such as I had heard from the roughest Canadian types? I was sickened with horror at the thought of a little girl, standing frozen and terrified at the mouth of the sea cave while her mother cold-bloodedly smashed the face of her father. . . .

Deirdre raised her head. "I—I couldn't say anything, I could only stand there, and then I screamed, I screamed and—and Mother saw me, she ran to me and grabbed me, I thought she would kill me too, and she shook me, she shook me and shook me and shook me until I was sick and threw up. . . . I threw up all over her dress, and she pushed me down and she kept saying to me, again and again, 'You must never say a word, you must never say a word. . . .' And then she dragged me into the cave and pushed me into a corner and she—she buried the box in the upper cave, and I—I guess I started to scream again, I don't remember, because she hit me and I fell down into the lower cave and—and I don't remember any more," she said, with a long gasp. "Then I woke up and it was night and the water was all around me. And Papa was lying in the water and his face was all gone. . . . And I screamed and screamed but nobody came, and the water was coming up and up, and I was so cold, so cold. . . . And I climbed up into the upper cave, and the water came up and came up, and I was afraid it would come up there too, and I sat there and sat there and wondered if Mother would come back and kill me too, and it got colder and colder until I thought I'd freeze, and then . . . and then I really don't remember any more," she whispered, and went limp in my arms. "The next thing I remember I was playing with my dolls and I had different clothes and Margo was with me and Jeremy wasn't a baby any more. . . ."

Weak with horror and reaction, I clung to the girl. There was no further doubt in my mind. This was the

176

solution to the old murder, then. And the shock of seeing her mother murder her father, the shock of being shaken and beaten and then—cold-bloodedly left for dead, or to drown in the incoming tide? She had suffered from shock and exposure; small wonder if the shock had turned her brain! And then, when her speech returned and memory began to return—there was Martine, attacking, continually telling her she could not remember, frightening her again into terrified silence and withdrawal. . . .

But now that we knew the truth, what could I do? Would anyone believe Deirdre's tale? How could I prove it?

Brant, the thought came to me with a helpless longing, if I could only tell Brant. But the memory of Margo came to me, bringing cold chills. Suppose Margo had found this out and come to him—and he, being in connivance with Martine, had killed her and shifted the evidence to Deirdre?

I felt alone, terrified, shadowed with death and terror. And the child was clinging to me, relying on me to protect her against this new and frightful knowledge.

What could I do?

Chapter

Fifteen

I LOOKED OUT toward the beach through the hole in the cliff. The tide was rolling in; already the strip of beach had narrowed to a bare three or four feet, and occasional wavelets licked at the base of the cliff. The lashing rain and wind beat the surf high and howled in the echoing sea cave.

I took Deirdre's cold hand in mine.

"We must get back, darling," I said. "It's cold here, and the tide's rising."

She turned obediently toward the entrance to the lower cliff, then, shaking, stopped and said, "I'm afraid to go back there, Susan! Now that I know it's true . . ."

I tried to sound firm and reasuring. "How will anyone know that you remember, unless you tell them? You're in no more danger than you have been all these years."

"But—some day we'll have to tell them. . . ."

"Yes," I said, thoughtfully. It would have to come out now. I thrust the damp letters into the pocket of my own raincoat. "But not right away. I'll try to get you away, first, to the mainland, where you'll be safe." When Martine was accused of her first husband's murder, I wanted Deirdre to be in a good safe place, preferably with several miles between her and her mother. "I'll see what Doctor Mason thinks. Maybe you could go and stay where Hester and Jeremy are staying."

"I'd like that," she said. "But for now . . . ?"

"For now, the only thing to do is to go back and to pretend that everything's just as it's always been and that you don't remember anything," I told her.

She started down the steep scramble into the lower cave, sure-footed on the rocks, holding out her hand to

178

help me get my balance when I slipped. What would this girl be like when, freed of terror and the memory of murder, she came sanely into the world of today? With all my heart, I would be glad to see it. She clung childishly to my hand as we came out of the sea cave and the cold wind struck at us, whipping our raincoats around our legs and blowing our hair wildly. A wave struck and rolled to the very mouth of the cave, and we jumped back.

Deirdre said, "When that wave goes out again, we'll have to run for it! Two or three more like that, and we'll be cut off!"

We waited until the surf rolled back, then dashed hand in hand across the beach. The next incoming wave caught us around the ankles with surprising force, almost sweeping me off my feet, and we clung together, soaked to the skin, until it rolled back again and we could struggle up in the wet sand and, our feet squelching wetly in the sand, make a dash for the path and the safety of the upper beach. We looked back; the narrow strip of beach was now a white-capped, swirling froth of water, rolling into the lower sea cave. Fifteen minutes more, and we would have been trapped in the upper cave until low tide again.

The castle walls closed around us warmly, seeming like shelter for the first time since I had been there. Deirdre was icy cold. I made her take a hot bath and get into pajamas; then I telephoned Mrs. Meadows to bring up hot soup and cocoa. When she came in with it, she stared at me in disapproval.

"Dear, dear! Wet to the skin, both of you"—she looked at Deirdre's sopping-wet raincoat and sneakers, which were lying in the corner—"and your hair soaking wet! You'll both have your death of pneumonia! Whatever possessed you, Miss, to take Miss Deirdre out on such a day as this?" She set down the tray, placing the bowl of steaming soup beside Deirdre with caution. She had brought, also, small frosted cupcakes for Deirdre and a pot of coffee which I was glad to get. The kindness of her motions as she handed Deirdre napkin and spoon belied the crossness of her words.

Deirdre drank the cocoa, and I saw the shivering subside. Mrs. Meadows, watching, said, "And by the bye,

179

Miss, that Mr. Hunter has been ringing you up on the telephone every half hour or so."

"Good lord," I said. I had forgotten Ross's existence in the fierce revelations of the day. "I promised to see him. . . ."

"You'd much better stop in the house, Miss, in all this rain," Mrs. Meadows said, "though he did ask you to ring him back when you came in."

I glanced at Deirdre, who was sitting up, spooning down her chicken soup, the pink color returning to her cheeks. "Yes. And I must go and change, too."

"I'll stay with Miss Deirdre, if you like. It's been a long time since we had a game of checkers," the old woman said, and I went to my own rooms, showered quickly and changed into dry slacks and a sweater, then telephoned Ross's cabin.

His voice was reproachful. "Susan, you promised—"

"Ross, in all this rain—?"

"I saw you on the beach near the caves with the girl," he said, "and you won't melt. It's got to be today, Susan; I'm intending to leave tomorrow. Can't you get out for a little while?"

I hesitated. Deirdre would be safe enough with Mrs. Meadows. And it would hardly be fair to let Ross go without a word. I promised, hung up the phone, then buckled myself back into the still-wet raincoat. I thought, *Maybe we should open up the secret passage; I could step right into Deirdre's rooms without going through the hall at all.* But it was her secret; I wasn't going to reveal it when Mrs. Meadows was there.

When I came back, Deirdre was lying on her pillows, drowsy and yawning, and Mrs. Meadows said, "I think she tired herself out, in all the rain and damp. She'll be asleep in twenty minutes, Miss."

Deirdre sat up and said, "Are you going out, Susan?"

"Just for a little while. You'll be all right in here, won't you?"

She nodded, closing her eyes, her fingers curling childishly around mine. It had been an exhausting day for the youngster—for me, too. I resolved that I would stay with Ross no more than an hour at most. It was early—it could

180

hardly be past six—but even so, an early night would not hurt me. And perhaps I could think out what I must do about Deirdre's revelation.

Mrs. Meadows looked with disapproval at Thumbelina, who was lying curled in the corner of the bedroom. "That great animal ought not to be in here!"

"Oh, let her stay, or she'll have hysterics," I said. But I was really thinking of something else—just in case Martine should have some idea of slipping in to her daughter while I was away, I could rely on Thumbelina to protect the girl at least from physical attack. Mrs. Meadows assented, grumbling. I bent and quickly kissed Deirdre on the forehead.

"Come in and say good night when you get back, Susan. Promise?"

I promised and went out.

It was growing rapidly dark now, and definitely wetter. I wondered, if this storm got worse, how Ross would get his speedboat off the island. I also wondered whether they had appointed a successor to his post at the bird sanctuary yet, and what sort of a man he would be. And as I walked, I realized that I knew Ross intended to ask me to leave with him and that I had no intention of going. I liked Ross; he had been a good friend to me, a welcome friend, outside and uninvolved. But in spite of the low flash point of sensual awareness between us, Ross was not what I wanted. For better or for worse, I was committed to see the tragedy of Sanctuary Island play itself out to the end. And it seemed wrong that Ross, involved as he seemed to have been with Martine—even though he denied it, she must have meant *something* to him—should be leaving now, before the truth came out.

I scrambled over the ridge of the shortcut to his cabin, remembering how I had met Martine here. How humiliated she must be now, knowing that neither Brant nor Ross wanted her. There was worse than that in store for Martine, I thought grimly, and then I could almost find it in my heart to feel sorry for her. For she was insane, of course. A bigamist, through her inflated pride; surrounded by luxury, but cut off from the world of her operatic triumphs; a murderess, probably in a moment of

181

insane impulse, forced to live with the living, breathing memento of her crime, knowing that her safety depended on the madness of her daughter and on her daughter's lost memory. She could *not* be sane.

The lights of Ross's cabin seemed a welcome refuge; and when I was inside, with Ross's welcoming presence suddenly all around me, it was almost a haven. He took my raincoat, put a drink in my hand, and led me to the blazing fire.

"I suppose it was selfish of me to bring you out in this damned rain," he said. "By tomorrow it should be a full gale, and we're right in the path of it. But I felt I had to see you again." His hand closed warmly over mine. The small, neat cabin, so different from the gloomy splendor of Duncarlie Castle, seemed to have returned me to the normal world again, as if I had come out from under a spell. As if in a dream, I let him kiss me.

"Once I get you away from the crazy place, you're a different girl," he said. "Susan, what's the matter? You look absolutely haunted. That place is beginning to get you down. You'd better get away."

"I can't leave Deirdre now," I said wearily. Then the exhaustion of the day rushed over me. I felt my eyes fill with a rush of tears. Oh, if only I need not enter the trouble that lay ahead!

"Is that crazy kid getting on your nerves?" Ross asked. "I wouldn't have a job like that for all the tea in China!"

Suddenly I knew I could not face it all alone. Ross was so safe, so *real* somehow, a part of the world I had left behind when I came to this haunted island. I said in a rush, "Ross, Deirdre's not crazy!"

He stared at me. "Wha-at?"

"She's simply been frightened—frightened to death! But she recovered her memory! . . ." Suddenly I was telling him all about it—about Martine's sudden, murderous attack on her daughter, about the shock that had brought back Deirdre's memory.

His face changed and grew wary as I spoke, and he said, "How do you know it's not just a new form of craziness—the kid making up a new story?"

"Because," I said, getting up and going over to my raincoat, "I have proof. Deirdre found these in the sea cave where Martine buried them, seven years ago!"

Ross reached for the letters, took them, and glanced over them intently. His face was grim.

"The damned fool," he muttered; "she should have gotten rid of these—well, I can take care of that!" With a swift, unstoppable movement, swerving like a gull in flight, Ross flung the letters straight into the blazing fireplace.

"What are you doing!" I cried out, then stepped back in sudden terror; Ross was advancing on me, his face set and rigid, the mask-face of a stranger.

"You damned, meddling, interfering little fool," he grated, "why couldn't you leave well enough alone? And I fell for that sweet, innocent little face of yours. . . ."

I cowered away, dodging behind the table, as Ross advanced on me. His eyes blazed with a rage I had never seen. Suddenly, too late, it flashed on me—the bond between Ross and Martine was not, had never been, that of lovers, but rather that of conspirators—blackmailer and blackmailed! Why else would a hooligan from the Las Vegas gambling tables stay here year after year, waiting out patiently the years until Martine should inherit all her millionaire husband's wealth—and leave, cheated, the moment she was no longer worth preying upon?

I screamed, but the echo of the beating rain outside was all I could hear—that and the inexorable footsteps of Ross, coming after me. Then something struck the back of my head and I sank into darkness, my last waking thought being, *What a fool I've been! Right out of the frying pan into the fire!*

Light struck my eyes. I tried to move and discovered that I was firmly bound, hand and foot. Behind me I heard a strange, repeated rasping sound, which I finally deduced to be the sound of a telephone being dialed.

Then I heard Ross's voice saying, "Martine? Anyone else on the line? All right . . . listen, and listen good! The whole thing's blown sky-high—yes, it's that damned meddling nurse. It's you and me now, whether you like it or not; so you're stuck with it. . . . We've got to risk it now. The kid? Lock her up; feed her sleeping pills again,

183

and this time don't get squeamish about the amount—
make a damned good job of it. If you hadn't left the water
to do what you were too squeamish to do eight years ago,
we wouldn't be in this mess now. You can leave the nurse
to me—another accident. And by that time you and I will
be long gone." He listened a moment, then said, "Can't
risk it. Don't worry about the storm; I've taken the boat
out in worse weather than this. It's all sky-high now." He
banged the receiver down, then came toward me.

His eyes stared down, blue, enigmatic, unreadable.
"Too bad," he said, almost in a whisper; "I thought you
might be the one."

"So you're crazy too?" I said fiercely. "Use your head,
Ross! You'll never get away with this!"

"Oh, yes I will," he said, with a laugh that was like the
scream of a wild bird. "What a shame you won't be alive
to see it. Who knows? Maybe they'll blame your precious
Brant for murdering you and the kid—and maybe even
think he shoved Martine and me into the drink, once
we're gone! The last survivor is the murderer in all good
mystery novels," he taunted; "so when Brant's left alone,
he'll have some corpses and disappearances to explain!"

And I hadn't trusted Brant!

I said, "You know you are insane, Ross—"

"Don't say that!" His face contorted, and he raised his
arm deliberately and struck me a hard, vicious blow. The
darkness rushed up again and swallowed me.

This time it was cold that woke me. I was lying on something cold and hard, and it was dark. I struggled and discovered that it was wet, cold sand beneath me, and the
broken fragments of a shell. The cold sea smell told me
that I was lying in the sea cave. A faint, precarious light
bobbed at the mouth of the cave, and I heard Martine's
voice protesting.

Ross's voice answered, "It's safe enough if we get going
before the riptide really starts! Come on! *Come on!*"

Martine said, "I'd feel safer if you finished her off
first."

"And have them on our trail forever? Hell no; she'll
drown when the tide comes in—and that's going to be"—

184

a pause—"just about two hours from now. Already nobody could get across that beach, not as unfamiliar as she is with the place. Let's go! When the water gets high enough to come up into the cave, the riptide is hell!"

I heard the sudden, chugging roar of a starting outboard motor, and I struggled wildly against my bonds; but the motor and the lashing wind drowned my outcries.

The tide was coming in—Deirdre locked in her room and forced to take Martine's powerful sleeping pills—and no one knew I was here!

Looking around, I could make out the sea cave and the darkness of the water on the beach. If I were free, even if I could not cross the beach, I could climb into the upper cave and wait there for the water to go down. But Ross had tied me with firm knots, and all my struggles were in vain.

What a fool I had been! What an infernal fool, to trust Ross! And why? Just because of a chance resemblance to Raymond Grantham? And I had distrusted Brant for no better reason than his bad manners, against all my instincts that told me he was good, kind, tender. And now I would die, and Deirdre would die, and Martine would go free, with Ross bound to her afresh by guilty knowledge. I did not envy *that* pair of maniacs their life together!

A wave broke over my feet, rolled up, and briefly filled my mouth with cold, choking salt water. I gagged, gasping as the wave rolled back. I had survived that one! But each succeeding wave would be higher and higher, until the sea cave was filled with surging, foaming froth. And I—I would be drowned in the rising tide! I lay there, rigid, waiting for each new wave. They came with tantalizing slowness; some of them stopped short of my feet, some broke to my waist, some rolled briefly over my head and back again; but every fourth or fifth wave broke over me, and I could not move. Sooner or later, they would not roll back all the way; already they were lapping at my feet.

Suddenly there was a new sound—a splash, followed by booming, echoing, noisy bark. A flashlight lanced through the darkness, and there was the sound of a scream. Then, as the wave rolled back, I heard the noisy bark again, and Thumbelina was licking my face and whining and dancing all around me, and Deirdre, sobbing, was bending over me and tugging.

"Susan; oh Susan!"

"Deirdre! Thumbelina!" I gasped, then gulped salt water again. The girl clung to the edge of the rock, trying not to be swept off her feet. As the wave surged back to my waist, she hauled me to a sitting position.

"I've got to get your feet undone," she gasped; "we've got to climb for it—up into the upper cave! We'll never get back across the beach! I'd never have made it alone, except for Thumbelina, she can swim like a fish, she gave me something to hold on to. . . ." She knelt in the salt water, tugging at the knots with her icy cold fingers. She was wearing flannel pajamas and an old sweater, nothing more.

"How did you get out?" I gasped.

"Never mind that now—oh, thank God!" The knot had suddenly given way; she jerked my feet loose. "Come on! Hurry!"

My feet slipped and I almost fell in the waves; Thumbelina, swimming, grabbed at the collar of my sweater. Deirdre grasped my hand and together, slipping and sliding in the darkness, we scrambled up the rough cliff face. We would never have made it if I had not remembered the climb from earlier that day; halfway up, Deirdre's flashlight slipped from her grasp and rolled down, with a disappearing splash, into the water. Thumbelina floundered up beside us, barking loudly

I thought of little Dierdre, seven years ago, making this climb against the tide. Now we were repeating it—for our lives! Ross and Martine were out struggling against the riptide, but I knew, grimly, that they would make it. Damn Ross; he always knew just what chances he could take!

We sprawled full-length, shivering in the cold dampness of the upper cave. She said in a whisper, "The water never gets up here. Although I've never seen the tide as high as this. . . ."

She was silent, and I remembered stories of monstrous hurricane tides, ten or fifteen feet above normal. If the

186

water came up here, we were lost. But there was no use in worrying about that now. For the minute, although we were icy cold, shivering, and drenched to the skin, we were safe from drowning. We clung together in our soaked clothes. At last, when I recovered my breath and courage, I managed to ask in wonder, "How did you get out, Deirdre? Ross said on the phone—your mother—"

"She came in," Deirdre said. "I knew something was wrong because she was—was almost nice to me. She said I'd gotten all wet in the rain and I needed a good sleep or I'd get pneumonia. I was already scared because you hadn't come back. She gave me some pills—she made me take them—"

"My God!" I whispered; "what did you do?"

"Took them," said Deirdre matter-of-factly; "what else could I do? I was afraid she'd kill me if I didn't, so I swallowed them all, and then pretended to be asleep. She went out and locked the door, and I ran into the bathroom and stuck my finger down my throat and threw them up again."

I hugged her, speechless. If this girl was crazy, I wished all my own children would be crazy like that.

"But . . . with the door locked—"

"Out the secret passage," she giggled, like a child, "and Thumbie with me. Then—I was scared because you weren't back"—the laughter vanished from her voice—"and I was afraid someone would find me—and I knew I could hide down here—and then I heard the motorboat, and I was afraid, but Thumbie started barking and dragged me down here, and oh, Susan, I found you—"

She clung to me, trembling, and I held her tightly. We were safe for the moment, though the lashing wind and rain blew little spits of salt moisture through the dark hole in the cliff.

It grew colder and colder—stiffer and stiffer. We huddled close together, hugging the whimpering Thumbelina for warmth. The night crept by on leaden feet; once or twice a high-dashed wave broke across the floor of the sea cave and dribbled almost to our feet, but they could come no further. After an endless time, grayish light began to break through the hole in the cliff, and we crept to the opening and looked out. The surging waves still

187

covered the beach, but the tide was definitely going down.

"It won't be long now," I comforted the shivering Deirdre; "then we can get across the beach. . . ."

The heavy overcast thinned only slightly. Finally, stiff and cramped, we noted that the water had gone down in the sea caves and that we could manage to cross the beach. We clambered down hand in hand, with Thumbelina romping and barking around our feet.

From the top of the path I heard a shout. "Susan! Deirdre!" Then, a cry: "They're here! I hear the dog!" The next moment Brant McLeod was racing down the path to the beach. He saw us, cried out inarticulately, and dashed toward us, catching all three of us in his arms—Deirdre, the dog, and I—at once.

When we had sorted ourselves out again and the first incoherent explanations had been made, he put an arm around each of us, saying firmly, "You must come back and get warm and eat something before anything else." He began to lead us up the path; Deirdre stumbled and collapsed, and he lifted her up, saying quietly to me over her head, "I thought I'd go mad with fear last night, Susan. I've suspected Ross and Martine of *something* for a long time—more than the usual nasty bit of work, playing around behind poor Father's back, I mean. I suppose they've got clean away?"

Deirdre suddenly twisted in Brant's arms and cried out, pointing. He set her on her feet, then said, "Good God!" and ran, Deirdre and I hurrying on cramped feet after him. Borne on the last waves of the subsiding tide, stranded high on the beach, lay the shattered fragments of a small boat. Silently, as I came up to him, Brant pointed.

I saw the painted letters: Phoenix.

"He always had too much confidence in his ability to handle a boat, damn it," Brant said. "And nobody alive could swim in that riptide." Silently, he shook his head. "Poor devil. Poor Martine. God knows they were a pair of—of murderers, but just the same . . ." He glanced out into the roaring froth of waves, shuddered, and closed his eyes briefly.

Then, resolutely turning to me, he said, "We've got to get Deirdre home, Susan. And then . . ." his hand

188

clasped over mine in a way that was a silent promise; he bent over and kissed me lightly before lifting his sister in his arms again. "Come on, Deedee girl, it's beddy-bye for you."

She smiled her pixie smile at him behind drooping, weary lashes. "Don't talk baby talk to me," she said drowsily; "I'm eighteen years old, Brant," and immediately went to sleep in his arms.

Silently, we walked together up the path and across the familiar beach. We knew we had witnessed the first step of a climb which might be slow and hard, but would now be inevitable: Deirdre's return to health and sanity. And we had only begun to explore one another—and I knew *that* was a beginning that would never end.

The thick clouds thinned. Through the overcast sky came a single ray of sunlight, touching the gray towers of Duncarlie Castle with light, and from the forest behind us came a tremulous murmur of birdsong.

The storm was over—and it was a new beginning for us all.

189